WHISPERING WOODS

Magic behind the mountains

by Diandra Linnemann

September 2016

Dear Jonquil,

Thank you for your tremendous
help in getting things right(ish)!
I hope you enjoy the book!

Diandra

WHISPERING WOODS

IMPRESSUM

Written and published by:

Diandra Linnemann

Ahornweg 13

53177 Bonn

Germany

geschichtenquelle@gmail.com

www.diandrasknusperhaus.org

On a wise stone I once read:

"Nothing is written in stone.

Faithfully yours, fate."

Prologue: The last fight

In his last moments he cursed himself for having accepted the offer. If only he had known what he was getting himself into! Blood was running from a cut in his forehead, obscuring his view.

Of course there had been no in-person meeting. These days most business was done online. When he saw the message pop up on his screen, he thought about easy money and agreed immediately. That was before he got a first glimpse of his opponent.

He heard shouting and cursing – depending on whether the spectators had bet on him or the other one. Rain was drumming onto the first tender leaves of the year, intermingled with the clinking of champagne flutes and a hiss that meant nothing good. The thundering pulse inside his skull framed chaos with a wild rhythm. He hurried to wipe the blood from his eyes, but it did not help. The tops of the trees remained shadows, the blackberry bushes around the ring dry and brownish tangles.

Again that hissing sound, this time somewhere to his left. He turned around in a careful circle on the soft ground. He had to keep himself out of the corners. His injured leg beat with an urgency indicating that more had been torn than mere muscles and tendons. Huge fangs had torn a chunk of meat from his thigh. The creature's poison was burning through his veins like acid. His mouth was turning numb.

A quiet rustling of leaves made him spin around, but he was not fast enough. The beast raced through the air, a dark menace, and wrapped giant tentacles around his upper body. All air was pressed from his lings. Next something sharp buried into his lower body. The pain eradicated all other sensations.

He screamed.

The beast's jaws locked around his head. Please, he begged, make it end! That was when he heard the faint sound. The pressure around his neck disappeared. The clicking and hissing left him with, as he thought, a sound of disappointment. The throbbing rhythm in his head increased. If only he could turn around ...

His life drained from him as if he was sucked down into an abyss. His body shrank and became irrelevant. The shouts from the people around the ring flared up and were swallowed by darkness. It was over.

Chapter 1: Meeting again

The spark missed its mark, zigzagged across the patio and set flame to one of the ribbons I had tied to the branches of my tiny apple tree just this morning. The flames licked up and went out. My fingers tingled as if I had grabbed an electric fence. Damn. For weeks I had been trying – without much success – to recreate Grete's elemental RAF magic. The only thing I had gained so far were blackened flower beds and a written complaint from my neighbors. I inhaled deeply in an attempt to tame my frustration. There was plenty of energy beneath my feet, I could feel it, easily available thanks to dozens of rituals I had performed in my own garden. I started another attempt.

"You have to feel determination, but no headless anger", I heard her voice echoing through my mind. She had made it look so easy.

The exercise I had set out to conquer was something that should not need a second thought: Gas-drenched twigs lay heaped into a metal bowl. Had I used everyday methods, I would have had a cozy fire at least half an hour ago. But I needed to know how Grete had done it, I needed to perform the trick myself. Elemental magic is a difficult topic. Mastering the energies is considered a sign of true supremacy. Not even the stars among the media witches claimed to be able to create a flame of a gust of wind from nothing. I had always thought that stories about RAF magicians doing just that had been legends – until I had met one of them myself. Out of all places she could have chosen, she was hiding at my mother's Witchyard, a refuge for the innocent and the prosecuted.

By now I had taken the first hurdle – separating the connection to the earth once I had accumulated enough energy. This was not a must for the spell, Grete had explained, but the terrorists had needed it to not leave their personal magical traces at the crime scenes. After all the bad guys had not been the only ones to use magic back then. The Special Department for Magical Crimes had been at their heels. In order to make their lives miserable, the RAF magicians had performed rituals at secret gatherings and locked the spells into their bodies to take them where they needed them. This way the detectives had had a hard time following their magical traces. And once I knew this was possible, I had been hooked. If they had managed to do spells without being grounded, I wanted to do so as well.

I shaped the energy I had collected inside me into a sphere and walked a few steps. The construct held, even though the outer layer of my energy field trembled like a soap bubble at the tiniest movement.

The next step was way more complicated. "Imagine fire – not a flame, but the essence of fire itself." It sounded easy enough when Grete said it, and her demonstration looked as if it was a breeze. I had burnt my fingers, my boots, lost a few strands of hair. And trying to guide the energies – once again I had shown how much I sucked at doing just that.

The patio door opened behind me. My concentration wavered, and the energetic sphere dissolved. At the last moment I managed to guide the energy with my fingertips to avoid disaster. It hit the bird bath. The water fizzed. Steam rose from the surface. Great.

"When will you finally give up?", I heard Falk's voice behind me.

I turned around, protecting my eyes from the spring sun with my left hand. "Never! I thought you wanted to go to the gym?"

"I'm back already."

Indeed. Now I recognized the sweat stains on his T-shirt. Most people would have lost their attractiveness walking around like this, but Falk … let's say, I would not necessarily admit it out loud, but it really did not hurt his rugged looks at all. I noticed his dark brown hair poking out from his head in all directions. "Do you want to borrow a brush?"

"It's called fashion." He grinned.

Strega appeared in the doorway and rubbed against his legs. My kitty of doom had her own version of attention deficit.

"Why don't you take the day off?", Falk asked with a skeptical glance at the steaming bird bath. "I thought the equinox was a big thing for witches." So he had been paying attention at witch school after all.

"Not that big", I replied. Yes, I had taken the day off, but only from office tasks. I did make my money as a registered and certified witch, but still witchcraft was not something I could just switch off when I was not working. "Besides, Maria and her paper messes are driving me crazy!"

"It might be different if you had not gotten everything upside down again."

"Is that the proper way to talk to your boss?"

"Don't forget, I have the day off as well. Coffee?"

Boy, was he getting rebellious. Maybe his makeshift bed in the living room was too comfortable. I should make him sleep on the floor. But coffee sounded like a great idea. The chance of producing anything but burnt spring decoration tonight was slim to none anyway.

Falk had set his gym bag down next to the door. Strega rolled around on top of it, purring. Something about Falk's smell made her very happy. I gave her a push with the tip of my bare foot, which she ignored. My toes were even to cold for her to nibble.

"That smelly stuff belongs in the washing machine", I reminded him.

"Later." He was already at the counter, fiddling with the French press. He definitely knew how to make women happy.

I leaned against the doorframe, crossing my arms in front of my chest. "You sure?" I knew that he was not best friends with the washing machine. Our living arrangements could be so easy – but I refused to touch his gym stuff. Instead I complained every time it stayed in the hallway, marinating inside the bag for days, or blocked the machine, or just remained on the clothesline for days. Well, that last problem had been solved. Ever since I burned a hole the size of my fist into his boxers during practice, Falk made sure his clothes were gone from the garden before I started training. Something good had come from Grete's instructions after all.

The kettle steamed, blubbered and switched itself off.

Falk grabbed it and poured hot water into the French press. "Maybe we should have used the water from the bird bath. It was already hot."

"Really funny. Washing machine? Now!"

He turned around and shot me an annoying look. "You sound as if we were married."

"Why should I marry a man who does not know how to do laundry?" No way was I going to touch that disgusting stuff.

"Fine, I'll take care of it!" He pushed past me and grabbed his bag. I caught a faint smell of masculinity.

Strega meowed and stayed glued to the gym bad as he lifted it up. She did not give up her spot even when he opened the door to the basement.

"Fur is dry-cleaning only!", I called after them. Then I returned into the kitchen, poured myself some coffee and looked out of the window. My hands were still tingling, and the sole of my left foot felt numb – as if I had tried walking over burning coals. I was frustrated. Maybe I would never learn this fire spell.

The street in front of the house was quiet. It was still three weeks till Easter, the holidays had not started yet and most of my neighbors were at work. Only a few cars were parked on the other side of the street on front of a few bushes. I had parked my car right in my view – even though it did not exactly count as a new car after all. We had driven more than ten thousand miles during the past few months. I told myself it was car training and good for the engine.

The garden gnomes standing next to the "Magic behind the mountains" plaque my secretary had put in my front garden without asking permission had taken off their scarves and woolen hats. They seemed to enjoy the sun between the first light green spears of tulips, crocuses and daffodils. The time of the snowdrops had passed already.

A burgundy Renault slid into the gap right in front of my car. I put my cup down, surprised. Wasn't that … what was he doing here?

Raphael and I had not spoken to each other in months, and the Christmas gift he had left for me still stood on the shelf below the stairs, untouched. I might have sent it back, if I had known his address. Well, this was a problem I could remedy right away.

My heart beat hard as I watched him walk down the path leading to my front door. He disappeared from my view, and the next second the doorbell rang. He had probably seen me standing at the window. Playing "No one's home" was not an option. I pulled myself together and went to answer the door.

Raphael's blond hair was just as short as it had been when we last met. I smiled. "Hello, Raphael! What are you doing here?" I could only hope it did not sound less friendly than I had meant it.

A door sounded behind me, followed by the quiet murmur of rubber wheels. I looked over my shoulder and saw Maria sitting in her wheelchair, questions plain on her face. "Is everything alright?" Her gaze wandered from me to him.

"I'll take care of it, don't worry." I watched her maneuver back to the office carefully. "I believe you have already met my personal assistant Maria."

"We met in December, briefly. You were not home."

No, I had been in another part of the country with another man, trying to solve a mystery. And shortly after returning home I had ended whatever I had had with Raphael. He was just too needy, with his ex-wife and his insecurities and mood swings. I simply did not like him enough to put up with that. "Is this a private call or do you bring business?"

"Business. And I am not here for you, to be honest."

So? "What do you want here?"

"I need to speak with your assistant."

"By all means, enter." I had to force myself to step away from the door so he could enter. What business did Raphael have with Falk? Curiosity raised her head. "Would you like some coffee?"

"Yes, please." Raphael followed me into the kitchen and looked around. He did not say anything about the tower of old newspapers on the table or the footprints on the floor. I really had to mop the floor again. Falk was responsible for cooking and took great care of his equipment and work surfaces, but apart from that he had not exactly invented housework either.

"How do you like your coffee?" Another thing I had not learned during our short romance. It had been over too quickly.

"Black and sweet." Raphael took the cup I offered him and drank a sip. "You've got a nice place."

"Let's talk in the living room. My employee is still busy." I gestured towards the hallway. At least the living room was kind of tidy. I hoped.

We sat down facing each other on the worn red sofa. I noticed the stains on the armrest. The soft spring sunshine emphasized the stipes on the window where I had messed up during spring cleaning. At least Falk had been clever enough to put away his blankets this morning. Everything was covered in red and black cat hair, of course, but what else could you expect at a witch's home?

Something thumped in the basement, and then we heard steps coming up the stairs. So he had won the fight against the washing machine after all. There was something good in every day. Maybe Falk would eventually detect his love for housework if I just waited.

Strega came racing through the door and froze when she saw the strange man sitting on the sofa. Her fur stood on end as if she had bitten into a cable. The sound from her throat was feral and ancient. It scared her so much that she jumped onto the shelf beneath the stairs, swishing her tail from one side to the other, making the dust dance.

Falk entered less spectacularly, balancing a cup of coffee in his left hand. He held a box of cookies in the other. "I thought I heard someone else."

"Nice to meet you." Raphael got up and held out his hand. He was almost a head shorter than Falk, but did not seem to mind. "We have met already, if I remember correctly." Of course he remembered.

Falk put down coffee and cookies without haste, smiled and shook the hand that was offered. I wondered whether they had this weird alpha guy thing going – whoever could press down harder or something. I looked closely, but could not tell.

"Sit down and let's talk shop", I interrupted their arcane male ritual. Still it took them another second or two before they followed my suggestion. Seemed I still had to work on that authority of mine. "Tell, why are you here?"

"I would like to talk about this with your … employee in private."

No way. "Is this about a job? Then you're definitely talking to me."

Raphael raised his eyebrows. Seemed he had not expected me to be this demanding.

"Falk works for me, and his contract states that he may not take up any other occupations without my consent." I was afraid my head would explode from all the questions running around inside if I did not get any answers soon.

Falk was clever enough to keep his mouth shut. We did not really have a contract. At least nothing written in legalese. He lived at my place, did what I told him – at least when it came to work – and got a proper paycheck every week. I did not know what he did with it – as far as I knew he did not have a bank account. Maybe he used the paper to roll blunts, who knew?

After a moment of thinking Raphael decided that he did not want to keep me out of this at all costs. "I am here to get his expert opinion."

"On what?", Falk asked

Raphael took a cookie from the box. A few crumbs dropped onto his carefully ironed pants. He brushed them onto the carpet. "Your experience with street fights."

"Wait", I interrupted him, "how do you know about that?" Those files should have been sealed and lost.

Raphael turned around to face me. "You remember, during our first date, how we agreed to not talk about our jobs?"

I nodded.

"Well, I am head of a special unit dealing with magic-based crimes. Hence I get information that is not easily accessible for most people."

The wheels started turning in my head. "So you know Radinger?"

He nodded. "I took over when he resigned."

Also Radinger was the guy who got me started on my career path. His special unit had picked me up when I was trying to pull a new trick on a street gang. Instead of sending me to prison, they had convinced me to study magic at our local university. The rest, as they said, was history. I had not thought about any of this in ages. And most of all …

"Does that mean you know my file?"

Raphael nodded. "I had to know who we are cooperating with."

Well, I thought he should have told me when we first met. Which means there would have been no second date. My stomach felt weird. What a son of a bitch …

"But that is not why I'm here today." He pulled a brown envelope from the inner pocket of his black jacket and threw it down on the table in front of Falk. "Would you be so kind to look at this?"

Falk did not move. "This was not part of the deal. When my service at the Wandering Graveyard ended, my file was supposed to be wiped clean." He frowned.

"It is", Raphael insisted.

"Only not really", I suggested.

His gaze gave him away.

"He's probably wrestling that dreaded data bear. How does that get along with my right of privacy, or the latest data protection act?"

"This is not the question right now", Raphael interfered. "All I need from you, Falk, is to look at these pictures and to tell me if you notice anything familiar?"

I do not know whether I would have opened the envelope. Curiosity is one of my worst character traits, but I am definitely more stubborn than curious. Only this time it was not my decision, but Falk's. He tore the paper open with his thumbnail and pulled the pictures out.

I waited for him to take in the details. He took his time, then threw the photos onto the coffee table with the images facing the room. I bent closer and saw the pale face of a man who was definitely not sleeping. His eyes were clouded already, and a tear gaped on his forehead. Someone had torn out his hair in bushels, and foam was sitting on his blue lips.

"What are these supposed to tell me?", Falk asked.

"Do you know this man?"

"Maybe."

"He was a streetfighter, like you."

"That was years ago, as you know. I haven't been in contact with the scene in years. People come and go all the time."

"Have you seen similar injuries?"

"Even in the mirror, yes. Everyone gets their share of bruises. But these pictures do not show why he died, am I right?"

Raphael pulled another image from his pocket and put it on top of the other images with careful movement. "We think this was the fatal wound."

I looked away quickly. Ouch. Yes, that might have been the one. The guy's lower abdomen was ripped open, the edges of the wound black and frayed. His intestines had slipped from their cavity and lay gleaming on the wet grass.

"You can't do that with your bare hands", Falk stated matter-of- fact. "I never got involved in weapons."

"This was not done with a weapon – at least none that our experts know. In addition we found an unknown chemical agent in the dead man's blood. This is what caused the discoloration."

"Do you know who he is?", I asked. Some part of me did not want to know a name, or any other details. Some other part was fascinated in a scary way. I was getting used to images like these.

18

"Dimitri Kosarow, a young star in the streetfighter circus. At least until three days ago", Raphael said. "We asked family and friends, but of course they don't know a thing. Obviously he went to church every Sunday."

"Didn't help." Falk took the picture into his hands and gave it a closer look. "So you think he died during a fight?"

"We are pretty sure. Besides the injuries demonstrated here, he had numerous fractures and bruises. And he made a major deposit just a week ago. My men assume this was the advance payment."

Falk made a face. "That's why I don't have a bank account. Not enough privacy."

Maybe I should get rid of mine as well. It started to look as if our privacy was not in the best hands around here.

Falk handed the picture back to Raphael. "Sorry, I have nothing I could tell you that you don't know already."

"The information is not the main reason I am here."

Really?

"I would like to ask you to act as our contact inside the organization."

Wait, what? I put my cup down with a thunk. "You must be out of your mind."

Falk held up his hands to stop me. "I want to know what he has to offer."

Raphael acted as if I was not even there. He turned towards Falk. "We need someone who won't look out of place in this environment."

I was not going to be silenced this easily. "Someone to get beat up in your place, you mean."

They kept ignoring me. Falk said, "If I do this, you are going to wipe my files clean once and for good. Immaculate, without exceptions."

"We could do that."

"No could, no talking. Just do it."

"Do we have a deal?" Raphael got up and walked around the table towards the hallway.

Falk followed him. "How do I contact this organization?"

"Don't trouble yourself, we have already made arrangements", Raphael replied.

That puny confident runt. My fingertips tingled. I looked down at my hands and noticed tiny burn marks on the red cushions. Damn! Quickly I closed my fists and took a few careful deep breaths.

The men shook hands again, cementing their agreement. Seemed as if I had missed the details. I jumped off the sofa, hit my knee against the glass surface of the table and spilled coffee from the cups. "Wait a moment!"

Both looked at me as if I was interfering with grownup business. That did not stop me. "You said your department thinks this is about magic. And then you send Falk into the lion's den? That's madness! He is not a wizard!"

"I do know how to take care of myself."

In that moment I would have loved to punch him. "Raphael, as his boss I have to insist to take a closer look at the body before anything else happens."

He frowned. "What do you hope to find there? I've put my best people on it."

His best people, what did that mean? They were not me. And when it came to magic, my own powers were what I preferred to rely on. "Is the crime scene still cordoned off?"

"Yes", he answered reluctantly, as if I was keeping him from doing important stuff.

"Then I will go and take a look. Maybe I can find something your people have missed." I swallowed my pride, "You know my file, hence you know I am not any run-off-the-mill witchling."

"And if I agree, you will let your assistant play with the big boys?"

Wait, was he making fun of me? "Maybe."

"I guess that's your best offer." Raphael's gaze wandered from me to Falk and back. "I think it best if we go there right away."

I looked at Falk, nodded. Then I called, "Maria, we have to leave. Please lock the door when you're leaving."

The rustling of papers in my office stopped. A moment later my personal assistant appeared in the doorway, almost without a sound. She maneuvered her wheelchair around the corkscrew stairs with her usual ease. She had probably overheard most of what we had been talking about.

I saw in Raphael's face how he followed the same train of thought. "Has she been eavesdropping?"

"I'm just a cripple, not deaf", Maria replied and threw her black hair back over her shoulder with an angry jerk of her head. "I would greatly appreciate it if you addressed me directly. And no, I was listening to music." She pulled her ipod from her pocket. The white earphones dangled next to her wheelchair and immediately attracted Strega's attention. The cat dropped off the shelf and started stalking the white plastic buttons.

"Strega, stop!" I smiled. "Raphael, have you forgotten that you talked to Maria only minutes ago?"

A red flush rose from the collar of his shirt. "Excuse my bad manners. Nevertheless, I have to inform you that everything that was discussed in this house today is strictly confidential."

"Never mind, who would want to talk with a cripple like me?" Yes, Maria was enjoying his embarrassment. She was definitely not a shy wilting flower.

Which reminded me of something else. "Here, I never got around to giving it back to you." I grabbed the holiday present off the shelf and handed it to Raphael. He looked surprised. "Thanks for your consideration, but I think you should take it with you again." Then I turned around to Maria. "You'll get home safely?"

"Sure, why not? Weather is great, I'll take the shortcut through the park." She maneuvered past us towards the main door. I heard the cloth of her jacket rustling, followed by the clicking of the lock. "See you tomorrow!", she called from the front garden.

"You should follow me in your car", Raphael stated matter-of-fact. He held the wrapped gift as if it was explosive.

Well, we could always get back to the mess in the living room later. I glanced at Falk – I had no idea what he thought about me interfering. Ah well, I did not really care. After all I still was the boss.

Chapter 2: Signs of a struggle

It was late afternoon, and traffic on the main street stuck like fresh jam sticking to a wooden spoon. We passed the tunnel under the city in slow motion. The first traces of evening rush-hour crept from one traffic light to the next, most drivers with an annoyed expression and their mobiles pressed between shoulder and ear. This was against the law, but no one sweats the small stuff when it comes to traffic.

We parked next to a fishkeeping shop which I had been seeing from the window of my car in passing for years. I did not know how it could stay open. A stick-like man with glasses looked at us without joy from behind the cashier. Having the police nearby did not make him happy. We probably ruined his last shreds of business. Several police cars were parked below the stuffed front window. The blue and grey cars gleamed in the sunlight. I still had not gotten used to the new design, it had only been around, what, ten years? Still it was pretty. I waited for two bicycles to pass me, parked my car next to Raphael's and switched off the engine.

The day was cold and windy. We were standing at a four-lane street with a line of bare trees on the other side. Behind the trees a cargo train passed. I snuggled into the collar of my grey woolen coat and followed Falk, who in turn was following Raphael. Seemed he wanted to get a whiff of my line of work. I did not mind, maybe he would even learn something useful.

Next to the fishkeeping shop there was a plot of land that had originally been supposed to become a building site. These days it looked more like a birch grove, with plenty of slender trees reaching towards the sky with white and silver limbs, ending in purple and black feathery twigs. At the edge of the area yellowish grass seemed to dream of last year's spring. Clouds of blackberry bushes had started conquering the open space. Empty crisp packages and broken beer bottles littered the ground. This looked like a fancy spot for teenagers to get drunk and sniff exhaust fumes. Yuck.

Heavy police boots had tread a path right through the underbrush. Thornes grabbed for my coat. I tugged at the cloth. Something whispered in the pit of my stomach. The engine song at my back grew quieter. Another train rushed past, towards the main station.

Although the body had been moved already, the place where it had been found was easy to make out. First of all there were plenty of police officers and specialists in plain clothes milling around. Second, there was this smell. The body must have had time to ripen despite the low temperatures, and the fluids released by decay had seeped into the ground. I wrinkled my nose.

Falk stopped next to Raphael, offering greetings to the people waiting. No one dared question his presence. Or maybe they were used to having civilians around. What did I know about policework?

"Helena? What a lovely surprise!"

I stopped and looked around. Who at a crime scene would be this glad to see me? I thought I remembered the voice, but it must have been years ago.

A stocky guy with glasses, carrot-colored short hair and a freckled grin walked towards me. "Don't you remember me? It's me, Patrick! We used to sit next to each other during Magic History lessons!"

Now that he mentioned it … "Surprise indeed! Blessed Ostara!", I replied. Indeed, I was glad to see him. We had not exactly been friends to be sure, but in hindsight those had been great days, and Patrick had been one of my buddies. Sometimes we had shared beer and donuts while learning, especially all that theoretical stuff I could not wrap my mind around. He was from a wealthy family in the south who had cut him out of their will when he decided to study magic, and he had never even attempted to flirt with me. A great fellow. "What are you doing here?"

"Working for the authorities", he explained with pride. "My grades were not quite as good as yours, but as you are freelancing, there was hardly any competition."

I pointed at his white overalls. "Is that official work gear or only the next generation of your sweatpants collection?"

He snorted. "You know, I still have that green one you always ogled me in." With a grin he added, "You didn't think I'd notice, right?"

"Oh no!", I joked. "You found me out!" It was easy to fall back into familiar patterns – just for one moment. Then I became serious. "Raphael said I could look at the place where they found the body."

"Yeah, he told us to not touch anything until you arrived."

How nice of him – wait, what? Had he expected me to interfere? What a prick.

"This way." Patrick turned on his heel and walked down the path he had come on. "We have found nothing unusual – no signs of a ritual, no energetic traces. The

26

substance found in the dead man's blood stream seems to be a dead end. Maybe some fancy neurotoxin, maybe a new drug, the lab isn't sure. We have no information on the chemical compounds yet."

"Does that happen regularly?"

"More often than we would like. We're doing our best to keep up to date. Have to know what's hip with the kids."

I stopped. "Patrick, look at me."

He turned around with confusion written across his face. "What?"

"No one says 'hip' or 'kids' anymore."

"My goodness!" He covered his mouth with his hand. "I am turning into Auntie Yvonne!"

"Does that mean you'll finally grow a beard?" I had not known I could be this witty. Maybe I should warm up old friendships every now and again – just to see what happens.

The smell grew stronger the closer we came to the place where the body had been found. I took my surroundings in with all my senses. Patrick was right, there was nothing out of the ordinary to be found. No symbols in the trees or on the ground, no ribbons, no energetic markings. This was just a normal crime scene. Some blades of grass were discolored as if they had been dipped into some sticky fluid. I hunched down to take a closer look. "May I touch?"

"I didn't know you were this shy." Then Patrick turned serious. "The colleagues are done taking samples, be my guest." He pulled a pair of latex gloves from a pocket of his overall. "Take these. Until we know what it is …"

"No bodily fluids?"

"I thought you'd never ask!"

Well, his sense of humor was starting to get on my nerves. Maybe that was why I had never called him.

Patrick watched me while my fingers inched closer to the stained grass.

I listened on the inside. Patrick's energy was hovering around me like a satisfied mist. He was easy to ignore. Faintly I sensed the police in the distance, waiting, Falk among them. Then there was the stream of cars and the railway right next to it, lines of steel cutting through the power of the city. To the other side of the place I could feel the quiet hum of the river. Quickly I touched hundreds of people, all entwined in everyday life and not at all aware of the energy connecting us to each other. Equinox made it easy for me to stretch this far beyond my own physical perception, and to grow closer to society just a bit. Only when I felt the connection to my own core growing thin like spun sugar did I ground with a few deep breaths and concentrated on the task at hand. So far I had found nothing out of place.

The body had left an echo. It happened sometimes, even when the dead were not found where they had died. I sensed confusion and sadness, which was to be expected. Next was pain from my ribs to my pubic bone in a sharp arch, dripping into my legs. The experience made me want to slam my shields shut, but I resisted, closing my left hand to a fist and opening it again. Breathing. Behind my shields I would not find a damn thing. So I kept breathing through the pain and continued to look.

The stained grass seemed to vibrate under my hand. Whatever had discolored them did not stick to the surface, but had seeped into the cells instead. I brushed my thumb over the surface of a wide blade of grass. The plant was not pale green or yellowish, as you might expect at this time of the year, but bluish-black. The vibration did not react to my touch, did not move in reaction to my energy. No ritual. I looked at Patrick. "What is this humming about?"

"What humming?" He extended a gloved hand and grabbed another stained leaf. Frowned, concentrating. "Have you found something? I can't feel it."

Someone else might have brushed aside and claimed they were just imagining things. But I knew what I was sensing, and this was not normal. "It may be very subtle, but the grass feels weird."

"Do you think someone performed a ritual here?"

"Unlikely, no one cleans up like this. But something is strange." I got up and heard my knees pop. "You should have the grass analyzed at the lab, you will find more than bodily fluids. And tell your colleagues to not touch it without gloves." This warning was not for Patrick, who knew the history of potions and zombie powders as well as I did.

We walked back to the others. Raphael looked up as we came closer and interrupted his discussion with a colleague. "Found anything?"

I saw Falk standing a few steps from the group, happy with himself and the world around him. I could only hope I would not get him in trouble by agreeing to this job. Don't be silly, I scolded myself, he is a man grown – if he thought it was too dangerous, he would refuse. Or that was what I told myself. Still the queasy feeling remained.

Raphael was still looking at me expectantly. I coughed and sensed what was inside of me. The further we walked from where the dead had been found, the weaker the pain had grown. I felt it like a memory. "Nothing explicit. The grass under the body is discolored and contains some strange kind of energy, but nothing I have met before." I grabbed his arm and dragged him a few steps away from the others. Patrick understood the hint and remained behind. "Why is your department involved in this case? To me this all looks normal enough, except for the grass."

"That's why we have kept it quiet. The dead man is the fourth one in three months whom we found under similar conditions. They were all exceptionally well-trained men, street fighters. And the exact manner of death was not determined in any of these cases."

"And what if I tell you that one of the bodies was found with the head removed – without any signs of use of tools?"

Now we were getting somewhere. "Just keep in mind that the media keep calling for pyres every time a child goes missing. It doesn't make my job any easier."

"Same for us. If we followed up on any complaint blaming magic for a flowerbed spoiled by rain or for a scratched car, we would spend all days chasing our own tail."

He had a point. "I'm surprised nothing has been in the papers about this whole thing. Usually they are not this shy."

"Obviously not a good story." Raphael smiled without joy. "Also we have a great legal department. No one wants to get in our way while we're working."

"What about the public's right to information?"

"What good would it be? Do you think some meathead reads this and decides to stay at home knitting instead of making money?

"Either that, or you'll find someone who has seen something."

"Tell me – did you know about street fighting? Before you met Falk?"

I shook my head. He was probably right, this would be scary rather than informational for the average citizen. Let the papers print the eleventh home story about our mayor instead. He was a nice guy after all.

"Has Patrick missed anything?", Raphael interrupted my train of thought.

"The energy stuck in the grass is rather subtle. I am not sure whether he missed it or just thought it was irrelevant. Maybe it doesn't even have anything to do with your case."

"Too bad you never decided to join the department. Rading kept singing your praise."

Did he? "I hate paperwork." Besides, police and the likes were chronically suspicious, even towards their own magic folk. As freelancing witch my life was much simpler. Why should I want to change that?

We returned to the group. Walking towards them I wondered what all those people were doing at the crime scene. Most looked kind of bored. Then again, what did I know about police work? And Patrick had said they had been waiting for me.

"Found anything?", Falk asked, closing the distance.

Shaking my head, I replied, "All boring stuff, sorry."

"So what's the verdict – may I go and play with the big boys?"

Argh. Was he looking forward to getting beat up for a change? If only he had told me, we could have arranged something! I swallowed my bad feeling. "Yes, we're going to help with the case. But in return I want all available information before we do anything dangerous."

"I can arrange that", Raphael replied. "Tomorrow by noon you'll have all the files."

"So we're done for today?"

He nodded. "I'll call you about the organizational details. Got your number, you know."

Yes, I knew. I had given it to him myself, and he had access to my official file. At the back of my head I felt doubt gnawing. Had our first meeting really been a coincidence? Or had he planned all of it after all?

No way of finding out, I told myself, dispersed the ugly thoughts with a determined nod and got in my car. Falk followed and closed the passenger door. "What next?"

Instead of taking the fast lane back to my place, I turned left. Above our heads the sky was turning darker. Purple and indigo streaks reached for the horizon. A single star shone over the shoulder of the mountains. Tonight would be cold.

"Where are we going?", Falk asked.

"I could do with a proper steak." Traffic took up all my concentration. Bumper to bumper, the cars crept through the tunnel towards the city, passing narrow condos. An older woman with her head covered was walking down the sidewalk, surrounded by a heard of black-haired children. She said something, the children laughed and raced to the next crossing. There they waited, laughing. I passed them carefully, keeping an eye on the children. One of them looked our way, and I thought I saw a weird gleam in her eyes. Some of the Oriental immigrants had brought their own version of fairytales when they left their homes. Djinn genes were less rare in our part of the world now than they had been twenty years ago.

At the next traffic light I turned left again. The windows of the library were lit, some event or other must be going on there. The majority of cars continued to the suburbs, and we picked up some speed. The city could really have needed some relief, but where to build streets around town when all you had were mountains?

Several teens were blocking the street. I honked and sent them running. Sparkles shot through the air. I bet someone was trying to get their fairy friends into the cinema for free. I frowned. Still I understood – they kept charging the same for every ticket, even though half a dozen fairies easily fit on a single seat. You just had to put something heavy behind them to keep the seat from folding up with them on it. And still they complained that most people preferred streaming to going to the movies.

We found a parking spot right next to the station – thanks to the parking sprites – and only had to walk a few steps. The bright green lights led the way to the doors of my favorite location – perfect steaks and the best cocktails in town. I had tried them all.

Fortunately, Thursdays were rather quiet around here. The place was stuffed nevertheless. Even with the door closed the noise was surprising. From experience I knew that most people would leave once the main movies started. I pushed past the smokers crowding the entrance, went up a few stairs and opened the door. Falk followed me, stepped to the side and walked straight into a tiny guy in a white shirt. An empty tablet went flying.

Falk murmured an excuse down onto the waiter's dark head and tried to make room, but between potted plants, door and seats he had hardly any room to spare.

"Helena, it's been ages!", the waiter welcomed me and picked up the tablet. "Who's that giant?"

"My assistant, Falk", I introduced and took off my coat.

Falk shook the hand that was offered, surprised. When I hugged the waiter I could see the surprise growing from the corner of my eye. "Do you have a quiet table to spare?" I shouted over the noise.

We were guided to the only empty table for two, in a corner, somewhat safe from the noise and all the happy people. Music screamed from the speakers hanging over our heads. The waiter made the empty cocktail glasses disappear with a grand gesture. "Take a seat, do you need the menu?"

"Yes, please, and two cocktails of the week", I requested.

He nodded and became invisible in the crowd.

"I didn't know you were a regular", Falk said, trying to sort his long legs between chair and table.

The situation made me smile. I adjusted my chair and turned my head to read the announcement on the wall. Every week the bartender came up with a new, exciting cocktail, and I wanted to know what I had ordered for us. SPRING BREAK, it said. The ingredients listed sounded good. Not that I had ever been disappointed by a drink around here.

"The case is bugging you", Falk stated. Must be a clairvoyant.

"I feel manipulated", I explained. "He knew I would want to come and see the crime scene."

"It's not difficult to know that, you've got the curiosity of a cat."

"Then why didn't he simply ask?"

"Think about it", Falk said, ignoring my angry stare, "you've had a thing going on."

"Three dates and a few calls, so what?" I shrugged.

"Probably not that exciting, with that wild love life of yours." Falk's voice was brimming with sarcasm. "Maybe he thought you two would be – more?"

If he explained it like that … never mind. I was still angry.

Shrill laughter rose from the bar. I twisted my neck to see what was going on. Two heavily war-painted chicks in their mid-thirties were kind of hanging on their chairs, watching the people around them. One leaned forward to whisper something into her friend's ear. How could grown women behave like that? They threw back their heads and laughed, evoking the mental image of hyenas. I could only hope I would never end like that.

Our cocktails arrived together with the menus and a basked full of warm baguette slices. I did not need long to settle on a dish. Argentinian beef, salad and manioc, that had to be good. My eating habits had changed drastically ever since Falk started a vegetarian regime in my kitchen, so this piece of red meat surely would not kill me.

Falk leafed through the menu, back and forth. Well, taking a vegetarian to steak paradise was not my greatest idea. I took a sip of my cocktail to mask my insecurity. The pink fluid was slightly opaque and looked pretty in the dim light. Tiny pearls rose to the surface. The drink tasted of strawberries and mint, and not sweet at all.

The waiter returned. "Found something?"

Placing my order was easy. And Falk had found something as well – crisis averted. "I would like the baked manioc and the salad with feta and mango."

Sounded like a good choice. We also ordered a bottle of water and kept looking around while we waited for our food.

"So what do you make of the case?", Falk asked after the silence had stretched for a while.

I shook my head. "No idea. I am not even sure that actual magic is involved."

"I thought you said you had found something."

"Yes, but it was …" I looked for the right word, "… inconspicuous. It might have been there for a while."

"Still it would be a magic-based crime."

"Or someone was just attracted by the vibes of the place."

He grinned. "Where do you get your expressions – the eighties?"

"Let's change topics", I suggested. "This is probably not the best place to discuss an ongoing investigation." Especially since we had to almost shout to be understood.

That was the moment our food arrived. As by command, my stomach started growling. Fortunately, the place was too loud for anyone else to hear the embarrassing sound. We did not talk as we dug into our plates. The only sound was the singing of the silverware on the white plates.

After a while Falk gestured with his fork, "Isn't this place a bit too chic for you?"

I plucked the strawberry from the edge of my drink and popped it into my mouth. "I like the booze and try to ignore the other people."

He smiled. "Yeah, that's what I thought." He dabbed his lips with his napkin. My gaze travelled up his arms to the broad shoulders stretching his burgundy T-shirt. The cocktail danced in my stomach. Maybe I should stick with just one drink tonight. I did not like to leave my car in town anyway. This might not exactly be a ghetto, and yet … given the choice, I preferred my own vehicle to public transportation. And walking two miles up the hill was not really an option, either.

Slowly the patrons left, and the noise level sagged to a bearable level. From our table I could see the chef taking a break at the entry to the kitchen. He looked exhausted – the hungry crowd had kept him busy, it seemed. He exchanged a few words with the bartender, nodded and returned to his realm.

"You two need anything else?"

I had not noticed the waiter approaching our table. His dark hair looked as if it had exploded, and his necktie was in severe need of a new knot.

"Why do you have this much business on a Thursday night?", I asked.

"No idea – I'm just glad they are leaving."

I could sympathize. "Will you get me a Limao Leaves?"

"Why do you keep ordering that stuff?", he complained, "that one is a bitch to mix. And it's not even worth the trouble, without booze!"

"If it's that much of a hassle, jut take it off the menu", I smiled. "Say hi to your buddy behind the bar, he's doing all the work after all."

Falk ordered a Sazerac. Terrible stuff. The only good thing was the single giant ice cube they put in the glass. Apart from that – I would rather use it to get paint off the walls than drink it. "Let's go sit at the bar", I suggested as the waiter removed our plates. "I want to say hello." The hyenas had disappeared – possibly looking for prey at the cinema.

"Okay." Falk pushed his chair back to the wall and unfolded his long legs. As he got up I was reminded of just how tall he was. Having someone taller than me around me all the time was not that weird anymore. But here – the only one Falk would not have been able to spit on the head was the bartender, who was mixing the contents of several pretty bottles right now. One waiter ducked under his elbow, grabbed a tablet loaded with full glasses and hurried across the room without spilling a single drop. This kind of talent never ceased to amaze me.

"My goodness, these chairs are uncomfortable", Falk murmured as he tried to arrange himself on one of the bar stools.

I knew better than that and did not even try to sit down. Instead I put my purse on a hook under the surface and leaned on the massive wooden counter.

"What's up?", the barkeeper asked without interrupting his mixing.

"Everything", I grinned.

"Sounds fine. Need a drink?"

"Your buddy is on it. We just moved to annoy him."

"Good idea, get him to working for a change." He nodded towards Falk. "I've never seem you here with him before."

I felt heat creep into my cheeks. "He's my employee."

"Employee? Does that mean you're expanding?"

"I also got a personal assistant." As I said that I realized that I was indeed kind of proud of this development.

"That deserves a toast!" The bartender put two shot glasses down in front of us. "Congratulations, Miss Businesswoman!"

"Hush, or do you want to get me a close tax checkup?" I took a sip. Lemon, sweet and sticky and with a hint of heat. "Your latest concoction?"

"What do you think? You're my lab rats." He pushed the glasses back up his nose. The light flickered of his bare head.

Falk had watched our interaction quietly. He threw back his head and downed his shot. I watched him swallow. The alcohol spread through my body, I was feeling warm. Enough for today. I closed my eyes and followed the energy spreading through the room. The other people were happy, elated. It was impossible to make out a single sentence in the crowd. I shrugged out of my cardigan and dropped it on my purse. At first the air was cool on my bare arms, but only for a moment.

Falk put a hand on my elbow and leaned closer with a spark in his eyes. "You're well-known around here, it seems", he whispered. "How does your liver feel about this?"

40

"My liver says my doctor can take it", I whispered back. When I turned my head, our faces were only inches apart. I saw his pupils widen.

I leaned back quickly, withdrawing my arm.

"Too much garlic in the dressing?", he asked.

I shook my head. "Look, they brought our drinks." I grabbed mine and gulped down the amber liquid, almost stabbing myself in the eye with the stalk of lemongrass in the process.

"You won't have it easy with that one", the barkeeper told Falk without being asked.

"Never wanted it easy", Falk said and took a sip. "I like me a good challenge."

"Hey!" I hit him on the arm – or I tried, for his hand came up quick as lightning and grabbed my wrist. I felt bones crunch in his grip.

"You do know you have to treat your employees well, right?"

"You're talking about pets, not employees", I answered and tried to free my arm, but Falk would not let me.

The barkeeper started whistling a funny tune and retreated. He used all his concentration to polish his cocktail shaker.

I returned my attention to Falk. To his fingers, to be more exact, which were still locked around my writ. The air in the bar was humming with energy. It was no big deal to collect a bit of it and shape it into an orange sphere. With a flick of my mind I sent it racing up my spine, across my shoulder and into my arm, travelling just below the skin.

Falk never flinched. I did not know what he was doing, but the spell did not have any effect. And this time it did not disperse, but disintegrated and chased up my arm like an electric spark.

My insides contracted, and for a Moment I forgot how to breathe. The tingling sensation lasted.

"Why do you keep stopping me?" I whispered hoarsely. "I promise, it feels good."

Our gazes met. Falk was still holding my wrist. His eyes were the color of thunder clouds. With his free hand he pulled a few notes from his pocket and dropped them on the bar.

We left the place without another word.

Chapter 3: The morning after

Soft rain was drumming on the roof window over my bed. I had forgotten to close it last night. A cool breeze slipped through the gap and caressed my bare shoulder. I was lying half on the side, half on my stomach, and my hair was messing with my view. Still half asleep I tried to pull the blanket higher, but something kept it nailed in place. My head felt as if it was filled with cotton. And the rest of my body ... I froze when the first shreds of memory returned. Had we really ... ? Heat rose in my cheeks.

A heavy arm landed on my waist and pulled me around. Falk's warm body pressed against me. I could not keep myself from sighing.

"You're a bad, bad blanket hog", he murmured next to my ear. "Good morning!"

I remained still while I tried to sort my thoughts. His smell confused me. Images flickered through my mind – to quick to be sure whether these were actual memories or just fantasies. A brief scan of my body confirmed that we had done SOMETHING. Something really nice. "You've bruised me", I said in reply.

"Last night you didn't complain." He buried his face against my neck and inhaled deeply. "You smell fantastic."

This did not work. I had to think – oh, that was the spot! His teeth grazed the tense muscle between neck and shoulder. I bowed my head and pressed against him. Someone was awake, it seemed ...

The rain had stopped when Falk sat up on the edge of the bed and started looking for his boxers. I turned around and watched his muscular back. Nothing would have been more tempting than pulling him back into bed with me. But this was not possible. "We need to talk."

"Is this where you tell me we should remain friends?"

"I – wait – hell, what do I know?" I shook my head and grinned. "I would have to be mad to refuse a second helping of this."

"Thanks for the compliment." He stood and pulled up his pants. What a nice ass.

I sat up and pulled the blanket with me as I scooted towards the headboard. "Be a good boy and throw those out, yes?", I asked and pointed at the two used condoms on the floor. "We don't want Strega to drag them all over the place."

"Sure." He walked around the bed and into the bathroom. I heard the lid of the trashcan. Then he walked towards the stairs. "Whatever we should discuss can wait until after coffee, right?" He looked so incredibly relaxed. No surprise there. I watched his dark brown mop of hair disappear. A stupid grin tugged at the corners of my mouth. This had to end in a catastrophe.

A few minutes later Falk returned with two steaming mugs of caffè latte. I had barely had time to organize my thoughts, but he did not even let me start. "Here, drink this. And stop analyzing everything to pieces."

The coffee was great. "At least we should decide how much we want the rest of the world to know. Maria will be here in thirty minutes."

"Feeling ashamed? Or do you think she will want the same rights for every employee?"

This made me laugh. "I'm a grown woman, of course I am not ashamed of this. But still you work for me. Don't you think this might be illegal?"

"Only if you start paying me more."

"Don't worry, that won't happen." I decided to switch topics. "I still don't like Raphael's plan."

"I know."

"He has not mentioned how he intends to keep you safe."

Falk faced me. He smelled of coffee and faintly of sweat. "I've done hundreds of similar events. I'll be safe"

"My, and I thought the goal of these fights was to beat someone up."

"Yeah, only that won't be me."

That changed everything. "And if they learn you're working with the police?"

"How should they?"

"I don't know. It's just … I'm worried, okay?" My voice sounded grouchy.

"And I appreciate the sentiment." His face remained serious. "What would you do if I told you a job was too dangerous?"

"I would take your objections into consideration."

"Bullshit. You'd break my arm."

Well, maybe that as well. Damn, he was right. This was his decision. "Fine, do it. Just promise me they'll look out after your gorgeous ass."

"Will do. Especially now that you've finally confessed how much you like it."

"Don't worry, I like the rest of the ass just as much."

The main door clicked. We looked at each other. Maria had arrived.

I swung my legs out of the bed and raced towards the bathroom door in the nude. "Dibs on the shower!"

Falk laughed and fell back into the pillows.

The bathroom was so tiny that the steam had heated it up after only a few minutes. I watched my face in the mirror until the glass had fogged over and only shadows held my stare. Had anything changed? At least nothing that could be seen – except for the bites over my hip. Seeing those made me smile. The shadow in the mirror started turning pink. Hopefully this would stop soon, I could not run around with my head aglow like a fuel rod. These things were heavily regulated.

The hot water took care of the remnants of last night, and once I had dried the memory felt like one of those weird dreams you would tell no one but your best friend, after at least two martinis. I wrapped myself in a towel and padded back into the bedroom.

Someone grabbed the towel and pulled it away the moment I had stepped through the door. I squealed.

Falk pulled closer and kissed my neck.

"Stop that and get in the shower!", I scolded him. "And then get downstairs, I'll find work for you."

"I love your romantic personality."

I slapped the hand that had wandered over my hip and just a little lower. "Maria will be surprised that no one is downstairs to meet her."

"I bet she has figured out where we are. She's catholic, not stupid."

I freed myself from his embrace and went to the wardrobe. As I opened the door I was almost buried under an armful of T-shirts. Time to clean this one up as well. Spring cleaning, here I come! For now I grabbed a pair of washed-out black jeans and a fire-engine red top with a fringe of lace at the neckline. An olive sweater for the breeze. Even though the rain had stopped, the sky was still grey. Spring might officially have arrived, but it was a long way till summer.

Strega sat on the top stair and watched me critically. No surprise there, she had been waiting for breakfast for at least an hour. Poor pussy, starving like that. I went downstairs on bare feet, followed by the black and red furry plague. Her meowing would have melted stone, and I knew it would only stop once her bowl was well-filled. Her song was accentuated by my own growling stomach. Another one who desperately needed some fuel.

Maria was sitting with a heap of envelopes in her lap when I entered my office, yoghurt in hand. "Good morning", she chirped without looking up.

I returned the greeting. "Any appointments today?"

"Something to do with the congress center at two, your contact is one Mr. Smithers. And at six thirty Mrs. Birdower will come to learn more about her late husband."

I had almost managed to get the congress center out of my mind. The construction site was causing trouble. Riverton had decided that this was the prestige project that would return some of its former glory, but they were more than a year behind their schedule. The Korean investor was charged with misappropriation. I assumed that he had somehow brought the spirits of his country. Or it might just be a case of good old-fashioned mismanagement. Anyway the case had made national headlines and several people had lost their jobs over the question who had signed this madness. They had requested my expertise in a desperate effort to safe their asses.

Still it was weird that I did not have more on my plate. Maybe it was because Easter was right around the corner. "Put all things that need signing on the table, I need more coffee." A glance at the clock told me that Raphael would be here soon.

Falk smelled almost as good coming out of the shower as he had this morning. The thought was kind of surreal. A tingling sensation in the pit of my stomach told me that last night had not ended my fascination with my – assistant? Lover? Boyfriend? He stood in the kitchen and was breaking eggs. "I could eat a horse."

"Tough chance, you're a vegetarian."

"Horses are made of grass." He scrambled the eggs in the pan. I smelled frying herbs and onion. And right that moment Raphael's burgundy car stopped on the other side of the street. I went to open the door before he could ring.

The garden gnomes in front of the house seemed to enjoy the diffuse spring light falling through the clouds. Tender tulip and daffodil leaves had sprung up between them. "Good morning!", I called. "Can't wait for the mess to start?"

"I'm just here to pick up Falk. We have to get a few things sorted out before we can start."

"You can't just pick him up", I told him. Was he trying to get me out of the picture? "If these are magic-related killings, you will need my expertise."

"We have our own experts. What we don't have is someone with inside knowledge of the street fighting scene."

"Your experts are not as good as I am."

He made a face. "You're pretty full of yourself."

I had nothing to say to that. Of course I was convinced I was great at what I did. Otherwise doing this job would be pointless. There were plenty of people who thought we were all just playing at make-believe.

"Be that as it may, we have no use for you today." Raphael's face told me there was no point arguing. Save your breath, I told myself. I would find a way.

I led Raphael into the living room. Strega had made herself comfortable on the sofa and was cleaning her paws. Behind me I heard light steps and knew that Raphael was right behind me. "You can have him in a minute. Let's only have breakfast first."

"Kind of late, isn't it." Raphael sat down. "Did you stay up late?"

"Not particularly." I hoped my face would not light up and give me away.

That was when Falk stepped through the door. He was balancing two plates with scrambled eggs and slices of tomato. "From what I heard I've got an appointment?"

Raphael nodded. "Just a few things …"

"No problem." Falk sat down and started eating. "I'll be ready in no time."

"Would you like some coffee or tea?", I offered Raphael. My stomach was growling, but I could not let him watch while we were getting stuffed.

"Water would be nice."

"Sit down and eat", a voice interrupted us from the office door, "I've got this." Maria maneuvered her wheelchair through the room.

Raphael looked alarmed. "Wait, that wouldn't be necessary!"

"Why?", Maria asked. "Do I look too fragile to carry a glass of water?" She smiled at him defiantly. When she held her head at a certain angle, like now, her black ringlets fell over her shoulder like a waterfall. Today the contrasted nicely with her butter-colored cashmere pullover. The golden cross at her throat glittered.

Raphael did not know what to say.

I enjoyed his embarrassment for a moment, then put a hand on his arm. "It's alright."

"But …"

"No, it's alright. Maria is pretty capable. She can manage some water."

"I don't even need a satnav to find the kitchen", she joked. The smile took the fire out of her words. When there was no further reply, she continued towards the kitchen. The rubber wheels of her wheelchair made a quiet sound on the tiles.

"Have I offended her?", Raphael asked.

"Ask her yourself", I suggested. "Otherwise you'll just dig a deeper hole. And now relax!" He was really slow today.

Raphael obeyed. His face showed his emotions. I enjoyed all of this more than I should. Well, maybe I was a little bitch sometimes. Nobody is perfect.

Falk was smart enough to keep his mouth shut, but I could see the grin hiding in his eyes. Instead of making everything worse, he concentrated on breakfast.

Maria returned, with a small water bottle and an empty glass balancing on a tablet in her lap. She drove close enough to the sofa that the light blanket covering her legs touched Raphael's pants. With a dead serious expression she offered him his drink. "Here you are, I made it back."

Raphael's head had turned dark red. "I am so sorry, I didn't mean to –"

Maria could not take it any longer. Laughter bubbled from her tiny frame. "By all means, stop digging your hole! It's okay, you're not the first to embarrass yourself." She tilted her head and smiled at him.

Wait, was she flirting? I kept my look on my plate to hide my surprise. Not that I did not want her to enjoy herself, only … I had not expected someone like Raphael to be her type.

"I'm ready", Falk interrupted the play. Indeed, he had already finished his food off. "How long will this take?"

Raphael got up. "Two hours, give or take. Our experts need to explain a thing or two, and we have to decide on our battle plan."

"Wait!", Maria called after the men, "you haven't had your water yet!" Her eyes were sparkling. "Can't let you leave all dehydrated!" She picked up the bottle from the table and came after them.

Her fingers touched Raphael's as he grabbed the water. He smiled. "Thank you." Then he looked at Falk. "Ready?"

Falk nodded and grabbed his jacket.

The front door clapped, and Maria and I were alone. I crammed the last bite of egg into my mouth and got up to carry the plates into the kitchen. Time to get my own plan ready.

"Maria, have you seen my black notebook somewhere?"

"Which one?", she asked from the office.

I entered the room and started looking under open envelopes. "The black one."

"Do you know how many black notebooks you got?" She opened a drawer. "I have started sorting them by date – if there is a date in your scribblings, that is. Some overlap. Maybe it's among these?"

Wow, that was organized. And: Yes, I did indeed have plenty of black notebooks. The black backs stared at me, each with a tiny white sticker on one end with a date written on it in my assistant's careful handwriting. I had never settled on one kind of notebook, hence the drawer still looked messy. I grabbed one book that seemed to be from last September. Grocery lists, addresses, obscure lists of ingredients ... there was no system to my notes. I simply wrote down everything I had to remember in any given moment. Once a page was covered, I pulled off the top corner so I could always see how much notebook was left.

I found a cryptic recipe for spiced Mabon wine and continued searching. And indeed, at the end of the book I found a phone number and a name. THOMAS, it said. That was what I had been looking for.

Thomas was in jail at the moment, that was our work. I hoped one of his shape-shifting friends had filled his place and continued using the number in question. I wondered who would answer the phone if I called that number now. How did they say? Only one way to find out. I punched in the numbers on my old Nokia phone and held it to my ear.

"What???", someone barked in my ear.

Perfect, I knew that voice. "Lizard face!" I forced myself to smile, knowing that it would carry through to the person on the other side of the conversation. "It's me, Helena – wait, hear me out!"

"What do you want, stupid cunt? You're the reason Thomas is doing time!"

"Seems you did not waste much time mourning."

"Drop dead!" The line went dead.

At least now I knew the number was still working. I dialed again. "We have to meet", I blurted out before he could think of more obscenities. "I need your help."

"Drop dead, I said!"

"Either you help me, or I will tell the cops a few things I left out in November. I assume you snuck off before they found your stash of stolen goods."

He huffed like an angry bull. "Meet me at the highway bridge." Disconnected again. That guy had really poor manners.

So I had a date. The thought made me queasy. These people were the reason Falk had been relieved of his … "duties" at the Wandering Graveyard. The mayor had been convinced I would need a bodyguard to talk to the shapeshifters. And he had been right. Falk still had a long scar from our last run-in with the gang. Those people dealt in drugs, stolen goods, blackmail – and I wanted to ask them for help? I might have had more stupid ideas, but off the bat I could not remember a single one.

"That didn't sound all cozy", Maria remarked. Of course she had only heard my side of the conversation, but she was definitely not stupid.

54

"The boys are okay", I tried to placate her. "Poor upbringing, that's all." I turned on my heel, grabbed my purse from the floor next to the wardrobe in the hallway and found the keys to my BMW motorbike in a tiny drawer. Strega sat on the shelf and watched me with mild curiosity. "I'll be back in time for work!" At least I hoped so.

The bike had spent a lazy winter in the garage and had only come back from inspection a few days ago. I grabbed my helmet and peered inside suspiciously. One of my worst nightmares was finding a nest of spiders on my face while riding. But everything looked as it should. I bound my hair in a ponytail, donned the helmet and turned the key in the ignition.

The motor purred. Life was good.

It was thick everyday traffic, but I wove between the cars without problems. The wet asphalt was only slightly slick after last night's rain – not as bad as in the weeks to come, when Mother Nature would release her pollen army on mankind. If they couldn't slay us with hayfever, they tried to wreck us.

Instead of following traffic towards the city, I took the longer way around town on the highway – a temptation I could not resist. My fingers twitched ever so slightly and the machine under my body roared ahead. To hell with speed limits – if I interpreted them generously, I would not even be late.

To my left, the Post Tower pointed at the grey spring skies like a giant finger. I flew past it. The river disappeared beneath me. From the corner of my eye I saw a barge groaning under heaps of rusty old metal pushing upriver towards the mountains. I only enjoyed the view for a second, then concentrated on traffic and bowed into the next curve. I braked just enough to not be carried off the street. Uphill I went, the road straightened and I covered the last miles like a bird singing in flight.

It took me less than twenty minutes to reach the meeting point below the Northern bridge. As I entered the parking lot I almost rammed a grandfather in a high-seated Suzuki. I avoided the collision at the last second and curved around the ugly purple car. Of course he slammed on his horn.

The graffiti artist of the area had wasted their talent on the columns and panels by smearing the surfaces with tags where they could have left works of art. Magenta, yellow, blue and silver spray ruled the concrete. Someone had sprayed an old clunker without license plates. I maneuvered my bike through the parked cars. Several spots were used by a makeshift bus stop, for the High Street was once again closed due to construction work. I took the right lane and passed orange and yellowish condos between meager strips of grass. Nothing moved on the balconies.

A group of young men in black hoodies was wasting time between parked transporters. None of them appeared to be particularly friendly. They seemed to wait for something. Now that I was here, my heart jumped into my throat. I had not forgotten that their former boss had tried to kill Falk and me. There was always something to ruin your day. I was sure we could get past those differences and talk like grown-ups.

Sure. And after that we would fight deforestation and stop global warming.

I took my time to park the bike and take off my helmet. Let them wait. I needed some time to decide on my strategy – turn around and ride back home? Not an option. If

Raphael and Falk refused to let me play, I had to make my own rules.

Enough time wasted.

The men watched me walking towards them. Their uniform appeared cute and threatening at the same time – they wore frayed baggypants to match their hoodies, accompanied by worn sneakers. They also wore sunglasses, although we only had March. Not being able to see their eyes made me nervous. I opened my shields just a fraction to assess their energy levels. Everything looked harmless, though.

At first glance, shape shifters look like extremely normal people – if they want to. Back when Thomas had been the big cheese, these had tried to blend in as well. Now they did not bother anymore.

I knew Lizard Face already. He grinned as I came closer, baring sharp fangs. Two thin lines of bluish-green, glimmering scales framed his slender face. My gaze flicked to his hands – men, those were impressive claws. I had seen what he could do with fangs and claws. And I knew he was way faster than I would ever be.

His colleagues looked no less scary. At second glance the boy to the left was not a boy at all. He was incredibly slender – to a point where it was almost comical. His neck appeared to be too long, his fingers too thin. The sunglasses were too wide for his face, and his fingernails too long for male hands. They were pointed. He reminded me of a bird … a vulture maybe?

Could shapeshifters grow wings?

Helena, concentrate! I could not afford to get distracted right now. I found another target for my thoughts.

The third guy did nothing to calm my anxiety. He could only be described as bulldog-shaped. He stood on bowed legs as if his body could not carry his physical presence. His shoulders were broad, the arms too strong – and as he grinned he presented teeth to make a pitbull jealous. I swallowed. "What a nice welcome committee. I see there have been some changes. Keeping Thomas's place warm while he is out?" I knew I sounded cheekier than I felt.

"When Thomas gets back he'll have to find a new place. Time waits for no one, girl."

A true philosopher. "So you're the new boss?"

"Do you mind?" Lizard face hissed. The saliva on his teeth glistened.

"I don't care what you're doing here. You don't happen to know anything about street fights going on around here recently?"

"Cold coffee, that is", Bulldog growled.

Lizard face silenced him with a punch to his arm.

For a second it looked as if Bulldog would turn on his boss, but he restrained himself.

"There is nothing new about street fights", he replied. "Has your hunk run off to play with his old friends?"

"I am not talking about the usual stuff", I insisted. "I heard there is a new … sponsor, offering a juicy surprise to his spectators. Know anything?"

"Maybe." Lizard Face watched me intently. "But why should I tell you anything about it?"

"Remember what happened to Thomas", I said sweetly. "It's always better to play nicely with me."

He turned to his buddies. "Have you heard? The chick is threatening me!"

"I don't waste time on threats." This was a moment where I could really use Grete's fire magic. A spell gone wrong would probably amuse rather than scare them. I decided to take the safe route and reached inside, felt the humming of the highway above our heads – modern ley lines, indeed – and the river rolling through town just a few hundred yards away. Enough energy for a tiny show-off. I put my hand on the hood of the transporter next to me and felt a tingling sensation as the magic – how else would you call it? – flowed from my hand into the metal.

The headlights turned bright, blinding everyone for a moment, then went dark in a shower of glass shards.

"Stupid bitch!", Vulture called. "You'll pay for repairs, I swear!"

Oops, that one was not going to be a friend of mine. "Could we talk about the fights now, please? I don't have much time to spare."

Lizard Face appeared to be thinking. "Maybe I have heard something. But my memory is really bad …"

Really? I did not have time for this stuff. "Tell me where I can watch a fight and I'll owe you a favor."

He laughed, and dimples appeared on his cheeks. As he removed his sunglasses I caught a glance at his yellow eyes. I felt a strong urge to just turn around and walk away. Walk very, very fast. "Your favors are stupid, I've seen how they work."

"Why, did my lucky charm for Thomas not work?"

"He's in jail, stupid."

If he wanted to look at it like that … "That's got nothing to do with my spell", I insisted. "He was dumb enough to mess with a witch. What did he think would happen?"

The men looked at each other. Something seemed to happen. Were shapeshifters telepaths? Not that I knew of, but then my teachers at university had not covered a lot about them. Maybe it was simple male non-verbal communication. They did not talk that much to begin with.

"I have to talk to some people, it will take a moment. And this favor you mentioned …"

Oh, that had gone almost too smoothly. "Yes?"

"Better make it something really special."

That he could bet his scaly ass on.

Half an hour later, I had just arrived home and put away my biker's gear, Falk opened the door. He looked deep in thought.

"So?", I asked. "What's the plan?"

"Not telling, top secret!", he said and hung up his jacket.

Maria and I exchanged a glance. That was how this was going to play out. "We have to leave in a few minutes. You know, the appointment at the congress center with the Korean spirits?"

He frowned. "That's today? I have to take care of a few things."

"What kind of things?"

"Stop it", he said. "I had to sign all kinds of non-disclosure agreements. Don't make it any worse by asking questions."

"In that case you had better get the stuff ready that we will be needing."

"I thought today was only a preliminary meeting. Can't you go there alone?"

No way was it happening like that. I took a deep breath. "Listen, buddy. You may be playing with the police guys, but you still work for me. Now go and grab our tools, or we'll have trouble. And don't even try that look on me!"

"Helena, is this only about –"

I did not allow him to finish the sentence and ran up the stairs towards the bedroom instead. "We have to be gone in twenty minutes!"

Upstairs I did not know what I should do next. This had not been the most adult conversation. I looked at the messy bed and smiled when I remembered the last night. It was a quick smile, like a ghost. Would it always be this complicated from now on? Falk was not naturally a follower. I sincerely hoped he would not start this "Me

Tarzan, you Jane" game only because we had had sex. I was not sure that would be worth the trouble – never mind how much we had enjoyed each other.

My mobile rung in my pocket. An anonymous call, how I hated that. I pushed a strand of brown hair behind my ear and pushed the green button. "Yes?"

"Do you have to make such a fuss about a little bit of sex?" Maria's voice sounded faintly metallic and very annoyed.

I was surprised. "What – how?"

"A blind man would see you've finally done it."

Ah. "I'm sorry", I mumbled, "I guess we seemed very unprofessional."

"I don't care. At least I did not have to chain you two to each other front to front to make it happen."

And I had always thought my personal assistant was a good Catholic. Well, she had most likely given up on our souls long ago. Welcome to the twenty-first century. "We'll figure it out", I promised.

"And make it quick – the clients hear you talking like that and you can kiss the job good-bye." With that she disconnected the call.

Clear words. And she was probably right. This knowledge did not make it any easier. I sighed. The whole thing was even worse because we were fighting about a topic where Raphael was involved.

By the way, I still had something to do. From memory I dialed my mother's phone number and waited for what certainly was an eternity until she answered the phone.

"What do you need?"

Wow, we were a family full of warm and tender feelings towards each other. "Can't a woman call her mother?"

"Not if it's you." The escalating marriage dispute of one of her protégés had been the last occasion on which my mother and I had worked together – following necessity rather than desire. We did not get along too well. "Say", I changed the topic, "is Grete nearby?"

"You got along well, didn't you? It surprised me, to be honest. Wait, I'll get her."

I sat down on the bed and waited for Grete. She might be able to help me with a few things.

Chapter 4: Trapped

"We'll have to do something about your appearance." Lizard Face flicked his wrist. A switchblade hissed into existence out of thin air, it seemed. The sound echoed from the concrete columns under the highway. Hardly any cars were parked here tonight.

I took a step back. "What are you doing?"

"You can't show up looking like that. They'll never think you're my chica."

Chica, well. I pushed a bright blue strand of hair out of my face and frowned because the hairpins Maria had used to fasten the wig to my scalp were tearing at my own natural hair. Lizard Face – who in the real world went by the name of Josh, but no one called him that – had indeed managed to produce invitations to the next fight. Seemed as if these events were pretty exclusive. I would accompany him as his girlfriend – who did not talk much. He had stressed that last part.

I swallowed the comment wiggling on my tongue. Of course Lizard Face was right – if I wanted to slip past these people, my masquerade needed to be perfect. I had been photographed for local media so often that I had resorted to a costume and a magic trick Grete had taught me. Having a former terrorist in the Witchyard had to be good for something, right? She had told me to listen to the shapeshifters while we were out together. "They care more about their reputation than about you, so they will make sure no one catches them smuggling a spy into the event." And that was why I was holding still when Lizard Face came for me with his knife.

Sash! Like that, my new jeans had several provoking tears.

"I paid good money for that!", I protested.

"Looks much better now", Lizard Face decided.

His friends grinned.

The wig had been suggested by Grete as well. No matter how good your glamour, physical masquerade definitely helped. Except for fake blue hair I was now wearing – freshly torn – blue denims, a black corset and a burgundy leather jacket with more buttons and straps than should be allowed on a single piece of clothing. The corset held my breasts high enough that they might even be considered proper cleavage. On my way here I had repeatedly been distracted by my own neckline. A stupid way to get yourself killed in Riverton traffic.

Of course I had had to wait with the whole costuming until Falk had left. Over the past few days we had forced ourselves to not talk about his job for the police forces. Instead we made pleasant small talk, concentrated on our everyday jobs – and finished every day in my bedroom. It only made our differences worse. I knew Falk did not expect to beat the family curse: The male firstborn of every generation was doomed to die a violent death. Burying my face against his shoulder, with my hands on his strong back, I could not understand why he insisted on serving fate the perfect opportunity on a silver platter. Maybe it was one of those elusive guy things. I, on the other hand, was determined to do everything possible to keep him alive for as long as possible. We would both benefit from his survival, I was sure.

For this reason I now got into Lizard Face's gleaming black BMW with its glittering chrome decorations. The black seat threatened to swallow me as I slid into the car, it was this soft. The car rocked slightly when two of Lizard Face's friends dropped into the back seat. My official companion got behind the steering wheel. For this special occasion he had left his hoodie behind and clad himself all in black leather instead. Looked like this really was a big thing. The leather looked great with his blue and green reptile scales that wrapped around his neck and crept up to his cheekbones.

We did not drive off right away.

Lizard Face extended a hand towards me.

"What?", I asked, irritated.

"Your mobile."

Sure. "You think I'm stupid?"

"Do it." He looked me in the eyes. "Just making sure you won't call the cops while we're still around."

"What makes you think I would do something like this?" If everything went according to plan, the police would be waiting for us when we got there. Raphael had promised me that Falk would be safe at any given moment. Nevertheless … I hesitated to get my phone out of my pocket.

"What's that?" Lizard Face's expression lit up. "I didn't know you care about archeology."

"Don't laugh!" I looked down at my trusted old Nokia, then held it out to him. "Here, make sure I get it back in one piece."

With skilled hands Lizard Face opened the plastic and removed the battery. Below this he found the SIM card, which he took out of the device and made disappear in one of his many pockets. The remaining phone parts were dropped into my lap. "I wouldn't be caught dead with that thing."

If he said so … I put all the parts together and secured the phone in the inside pocket of my jacket. If he did not know that emergency calls could be placed without a SIM card, I would not tell him now. His reaction to my mobile vexed me. What was wrong with it? I looked in the rear mirror and saw the two guys in the back grinning as well. The engine roared to life before I could start my sermon on the short lifespan of modern technology.

We did not talk much while we were on our way. I looked out of the window as Lizard Face turned the car around under the bridge, accelerated and raced up the highway at the intersection. He did not care about the red traffic light. Someone honked behind us. Keeping my hands idly in my lap took quite an effort. I would have preferred to hold onto something. Not even the view over the river as we crossed it helped relax me. The sun was setting in the west, and the light passed through the car almost parallel to the ground. We turned south. I looked across the driver and out of his window to avoid being blinded. Like this, Lizard Face – Josh – did not look all that bad. He might have posed as decent human being. Except for the yellow eyes, the reptile scales and the tattoos. These made sure everyone knew he was a gang member. Another career choice. And once Falk had helped put Lizard Face's former boss behind bars, he had used the opportunity to climb another rung on the gang ladder. Clever boy.

We had almost reached the south end of Riverton, with my home lying across the river and up the hill. I could not make out my house from here. The corporate tower on the other side gleamed in the sunlight. I looked that way quickly and felt a pulling sensation in my stomach. That was what coming home felt like. Only I was not going home right now. I wondered how far we would have to drive.

Not that far, it turned out. The highway transformed into a poorly built street, and after a few kilometers Lizard Face maneuvered the BMW off the main street and through two roundabouts right next to each other. We changed direction several times, passing old timber-framed houses and left the village behind in no time. I did not know this area too well – as part of my studies I had been here once to look at the remnants of an old monastery nearby. The only thing left were a few walls and the altar area beneath copper beeches – an impressive postcard motive. We had examined an old myth about a ghost monk, but had found no traces of supernatural activities. Our teacher had not been too crazy about our paper. Turned out that every year at least one group went to examine this legend. I did not remember anything else about this place, only the trees, the ruin and the annoyed expression of our teacher when we handed in our work.

My stomach felt weird. How did I know I could trust these weird guys? They were three, I was alone – and for all the right reasons only Maria knew what I was up to. Still she did not know where we were going. I could only hope that Raphael's troupes would be in place when we arrived, as promised.

We passed green pastures and the former monastery. More recent buildings seemed to enjoy the warmth of the evening sun, spread out over a hill. Then trees and more hills swallowed the view. The car whooshed around a bend without slowing down. Then we turned left onto one of the parking places reserved for hikers. Despite the time, the whole place was stuffed with luxury cars. A giant in a suit came up to the driver's window, said something that I did not understand and crossed something off on his list. I watched closer and saw a short black cable disappear in his collar behind his right ear. They looked well-organized. The check did not take long, the giant nodded and sent us on our way.

Lizard Face parked, came around the car and held the door for me. The message was clear. This was his show, and I was supposed to play my role, starting immediately. Although we stood mere inches apart, I could not see his eyes anymore, for he had donned sunglasses. But he was smiling. I bet that was a good sign. One more deep breath to activate my glamour. Now there was only one thing left to do.

The burgundy leather jacket was unfamiliar and it took me a moment to produce the payment we had agreed upon from one of the narrow pockets. My fingers felt cold. In exchange for company and cover I had promised Lizard Face a special potion, which was now resting on the palm of my hand in a tiny brown bottle. Three drops of the potion in a cold drink would make whoever drank that concoction desperately want to agree with Lizard Face. I was quite certain that production of this stuff was illegal already. Now I extended my hand and hesitated.

Lizard Face was impatient. He tried to grab the bottle, but I was faster. "Promise one thing."

"What?", he asked. Annoyance dripped from his voice.

"Promise you won't use this on any unsuspecting women."

"Or what? You're gonna call a cab and go home?" He grinned. And he was right, I should have thought of this earlier.

"Promise, or I'll go over there and tell the nice giant what you were about to do – taking a spy to the event and everything." Of course I was bluffing.

"Do you really think I need such a cheap trick to get bitches?" Lizard Face sighed. "It's way too expensive for that, after what I paid for the tickets. Now come, I have bet a nice sum on the second fight."

I nodded and handed him the potion. The second fight was the one I was interested in as well.

Between all the limousines the black and chrome BMW looked downright cheap. There was lots of glistening metal, and most cars were either white or black. Two or three veritable red sports cars stood between them, and a bright orange metallic Porsche Carrera. Wait, hadn't I seen that one in the local papers? But the most impressive vehicle around was the steel grey Mayback we had to pass to reach a narrow path leading into the woods – I would not earn enough money in all my life to buy a car like that. Well, I bet they did not have any pretty colors, anyway. Too exclusive. The car, that was, not my taste.

The parking lot was made from gravel, and I was glad that my outfit included black boots with no heels. An elderly gentleman was walking in front of us, with a young lady on each arm, clad in sequin-covered cocktail dresses.

They struggled to stay on their high-heeled feet. Poor planning made everything difficult. Tough to look good when you had to walk like a stork in pea soup.

Lizard Face put his arm around my shoulder. I fought the urge to check on my wig and instead snuggled up against him. He smelled faintly of sweat. His buddies followed us without a word. "Smile", he whispered into my ear. I obeyed and tugged on the corners of my mouth. My stomach tingled. I tried to look around without raising suspicion.

Where the parking lot ended and the forest began, another broad-shouldered guy in black T-shirt and black suit with a cable running into his ear as well. Security was very important around here. The guy watched us as we walked past him. I giggled at an imaginary joke and rested my head on Lizard Face's shoulder for a moment. I itched to check the area for hidden energies, but I could not be sure whether they had their own energetic protections in place. I could only hope my glamour was not strong enough to raise any alarms.

Fortunately, at least for the high-heeled ladies in front of us, we did not have to walk far. First we heard the buzzing of voices ahead. Slender beech trees along the path, young leaves touching high above our heads, made the place look like a chapel. After a few steps a path branched off to the right and got lost between tiny hills. This was where the party was taking place. The first thing I noticed were the champagne flutes everyone was holding. They sparkled in the sunlight. Real crystal. No costs had been spared. Were there catering services you could hire for this kind of thing? Finally I was free to look around me curiously and saw suits, ball gowns and sweatpants mingling beneath the trees. A waiter with a flower-white shirt came up to us and offered appetizers from a silver tablet. Caviar and pesto on crisp white bread. I refused graciously. For some reason I was not hungry. Instead I looked around me and tried the see where the action was happening.

An older lady with a fur coat looked at us and smiled. "You have wonderful hair, my dear. If I were your age … Are you attending for the first time?"

I smiled, playing shy, and remained silent.

The old lady nodded approvingly. "A wonderful idea. And so romantic! These nights make me feel so alive!"

Alive, interesting choice of words. The dead street fighter they had found back in Riverton would probably beg to differ.

Next to the fur coat I was feeling out of place, but there was the other category of guests as well. A group of glam-punks stood a few paces up one of the hills. Instead of champagne glasses they were holding beer bottles. As I was watching them, a green-haired guy – or maybe a woman? – poured the beer over her own head and growled. The stiff green hair on his – or her – head did not move.

"Do you know anyone around here?", I whispered in Lizard Face's ear.

"Sure, some of them are among my best clients." He nodded at three young men making small talk next to a group of young trees. They were dressed as if they were heading to the opera, and not about to see other people die for their entertainment. Black smokings, white ties. Penguins with huge paychecks.

No wonder Lizard Face could afford that kind of car.

The path disappearing between the hills was guarded by muscle-packed, bare-chested men in black leather pants. They looked like poster boys for wrestling. Their faces were hidden behind white masks that left only their lips visible and expressed professional boredom. We climbed up the hill to their left, Lizard Face supporting me by grabbing my elbow. I wondered how one would do this with high heels. Did they offer a carrying service? On any other day I might have taken more time to watch my surroundings, but I had a job to do – and no idea how much time was left. The people at the top were looking down the other side with excitement. Some were balling their fists.

"Let's take a look at the show, shall we", Lizard Face suggested.

I gave him an evil look.

"What do you want? I spent a fortune for the invitation." He extended a hand to help me up the hill.

I ignored the offer, took one last big step and held out my arms to keep my balance. Last year's dead leaves were moving under my feet.

Lizard Face grabbed my arm and pulled me in to him. He smiled, but his eyes remained cold. He hugged me tightly and murmured, "Stay in character."

I turned the head in his direction and watched with fascination as green, glistening scales pushed through his skin. It was still wet. My mouth turned dry. "Sorry", I whispered back, smiled and let him guide me up the rest of the hill.

A person on the other side of the arena attracted my attention. Well-tailored suit, broad shoulders, hundred dollar haircut – and when I heard the laugh, I was certain. Mayor Sterling. What was he doing here? Shaking voter hands? Quickly I turned around before he could recognize me. I did not want to bet my luck on glamour and a costume.

We reached the highest place and could finally see the ring – a narrow cauldron made of basalt and forest ground, maybe forty feet in diameter. A few trees were struggling to keep their roots in the meager soil. This must be one of the old Roman quarries. A steel net had been spread over the arena – to keep the spectators from falling or to keep the beasts down there from climbing out? Below us, on the ground, blackberries and weeds were growing tall. Unless they were being trampled, as was happening right now.

At first I was not sure whether the person who was getting handed their ass to them was male or female. I saw long blond hair, torn clothing and lots of blood. Something white glinted among the mess – the shoulder strap of a sports bra. Street-fighting seemed to be a place where women were being treated as equals after all, and were beaten up like everybody else.

Or torn apart. At first I had not recognized the fighter's opponent – all I could see were spindly legs and overly long arms. Arms? Limbs, I corrected myself, and too many of them. The thing moved in a weird pattern. As the opponents separated from each other, my brain refused to piece the puzzle together. Instead I focused on the woman inside the arena.

She was tall, all muscle, and bleeding from at least a dozen wounds. Where most people would have had a nose, she was sporting a deep tear in her face. That did not look good.

Lizard Face huffed. "Damn, I had bet on her going at least two rounds." He crumpled the paper in his fist.

"How long are the rounds?", I asked.

"Two minutes. They have only just started."

Wait, and she looked like that already? How many people did they go through on a night like this? The thought of Falk made my stomach contract. Now I spotted a digital timer hanging from one of the trees. It probably showed how long the round would go. One minute and twelve seconds.

"That's a tsuchigumo, they shouldn't be all that hard. They are mostly used for shock."

Yeah, that might work. The thing under the tree shook and hissed and looked like a mixture of human and spider and was roughly the size of a German shepherd. It waved thin arms with claw-like hands and seemed quite agitated. One of the arms ended in a gooey stump. My gaze travelled around until I found a separated claw twitching on the ground. Tsuchigumos came from Japan, were considered pretty rare and were only found in one place in Europe – the Moscow zoo. I wondered where these peoples got their giant man spiders. And as I was thinking about this problem, the beast jumped at the woman. She tried to escape, but the tsuchigumo got her leg and pulled her in. Her scream ended abruptly. Blood pooled on the ground. Something itched at the base of my spine. The digital timer over our heads had forty-seven seconds left. A gong sounded. The fight was over.

"Shit!", Lizard face swore, "that stupid bitich!" He dropped his betting slip.

Two men with a wide black piece of cloth tried to corner the tsuchigumo. They were wearing white masks. A third masked person stood behind them and was playing some sort of flute. I head a thin, wailing sound that made my hair stand on end. Something tugged at me, made me sleepy. I leaned against a tree and closed my eyes until the vertigo had passed.

Something was humming above my head. I tilted my head back, blinking. Bees were doing their job, completely unimpressed with the party going on down here, and flying into and out of a gap in the tree trunk. Spring as an exhausting season for these tiny critters. I hoped the noise would not make them nervous. The ladies around here would not be too thrilled if they were stung and had their bejeweled fingers swell to the size of proper sausages. Hard to get your rings into the safe if you had to cut them off your hands first.

After what felt like an eternity, I ripped my gaze off the peaceful dance of the bees and looked back down into the arena. The spider demon lay sleeping quietly – or stunned – in the arena. The men were busy wrapping it in cloth, then put it on a stretcher and carried it away. A heavy steel net was pulled up with cable winches when they neared the exit. The man with the flute followed them with his head down.

The dead fighter was dragged from the ring by her feet. She left a trail of wet leaves. Where she had died, the forest floor was drinking her blood. One of the helpers kicked a few dead leaves over the spot. The tsuchigumo had ripped open her belly with its sharp mandibles. A rosy piece of intestines dangled on the floor. I expected a porta-potty-like smell, the kind I knew from the festivals I had attended in my youth, but there was nothing. Had the promoters found a magical barrier for smells? That would be an excellent business for butcher shops and the like. I shook my head to get rid of the distracting thoughts and concentrated on the task at hand. Looking around, I tried to find any sign that the people were affected by the death of the young woman. And moreover – Raphael had promised he would have undercover detectives nearby. Falk was not supposed to be in danger at any moment. And of course I had believed him, till now. But this was not a game, no sports event for bored spectators with heavy wallets giving them back trouble. These were people dying to entertain the upper class. The public stood at the top of the hills, nibbling appetizers and drinking their champagne. No one seemed to give a damn about what was happening.

Lizard Face gave me a gentle nudge with his elbow. "I'll be back in a minute."

"Where are you going?", I asked. I did not necessarily like him, but around here he was my only ally.

"I have to gain back my losses. You say your friend knows how to fight?"

I turned my back on him and looked down into the fighting pit.

If this was a movie, there might have been a presenter. Someone giving a charming statement on the upcoming fight. Instead the digital timer jumped to two minutes and beeped. As if on command, the conversations on the hills shrunk away.

Lizard Face came to stand next to me. "If it's any consolation to you", he said quietly, "I have bet on him going all five rounds."

Five rounds? Against a nightmare like the one we had just seen? They had to be kidding. My heart jumped into my throat when I saw Falk entering the ring. He was wearing denim pants and a black tank top and appeared completely relaxed. Looking around, he seemed to have all the time in the world. The dark wet spot on the ground did not give him pause. I tried to put myself into his shoes. The walls of the fighting pit were too steep to climb them without equipment, and of course there was also the net. The spectators stood maybe twelve or fourteen feet above the fighters. In some places the walls were perpendicular. Square basalt pillars protruded into the arena. Trampled blackberry bushes covered the ground, the leaves splattered with blood. Two young trees in the middle of the pit were still unharmed. They would not yield any protection. I doubted that anyone could climb them, they were too slender and too bare. In a few years maybe – but that was the kind of time we did not have.

A large box was placed behind the steel net at the entry to the ring. Something was moving in the shadows. I thought I could see thick fur. The last betting slips changed hands on the hills. Tension was rising. Falk stalked around the ring, increasing the distance to his opponent. From up here I could see his shoulder muscles work. Not that relaxed after all. I forced a long breath into my lungs. My fingers were ice cold.

The steel net was lifted a little bit in the middle, and someone opened the box.

A whirlwind of fur and claws exploded into the arena.

78

Falk jumped to the side, rolled over his shoulder and was back on his feet in no time. I had seen nothing, but a fine red line was running across his left upper arm. The first complaints rose from the crowd. Some had bet on first blood. I looked at them quickly, only long enough to wish they would get chickenpox. Right now I did not care whether this wish might come true. Where were Raphael's people, for Frigg's sake?

My assistant, at the center of attention, did not seem to care much about the way things had started. He kept moving, calmly, almost gracefully. His opponent remained motionless and inhaled, crouching on all fours.

"What kind of beast is that?", I asked Lizard Face.

"No idea. But if your guy wins I want that pelt for my bedroom."

He might just as well get a Galloway pelt to put on the floor. The beast was as tall as a calf and built like a sloth. A fast, angry sloth. Its front legs – or rather arms? – seemed to be too long for its body. Coarse rust-colored fur covered its whole body. The head looked like a deformed plush ball. This was why it took me a moment to realize something important.

The beast was blind.

There were no eyes in its face, or not that I could see, but there was a mouth filled with razor teeth. I knew it was a cliché, I would have liked to avoid it myself. The beast tilted its head and sniffed. Or maybe it was listening? Then it bared its teeth and turned toward Falk.

Damn, perfect orientation even in pitch black. Where were those stupid undercover cops? This would be the perfect moment to interfere. Raphael had promised that there would be no real danger at any point. Falk would be monitored using GPS and a hidden microphone, and as soon as the task force knew where the event was taking place, everyone would get into position. Not that I could see any of that.

The furry thing stalked towards Falk. He retreated and stepped to the side, so as not to end up in a corner. He stumbled over a hidden branch. My heart stopped. Don't fall, I begged silently.

Falk did not miss a step. He almost danced away from the basalt wall and led his opponent in a slow circle. The people around us grew restless. It looked as if not enough was happening. Boring without pints of blood. For me, on the other hand, the red line on Falk's bare arm was more than enough.

I did not see who kicked the gravel avalanche down into the arena. The monster did not see anything, either, but the noise ripped it from its waiting stance. It jumped at Falk, hissing. The sound made my bones freeze. I grabbed Lizard Face's arm.

Instead of retreating, Falk dropped on the ground. When the monster was almost upon him, he grabbed its fur. The energy of the attack was enough to help him throw the beast against one of the slender trees. He was back on his feet before I had gotten over the shock.

The beast howled with frustration. It leapt to its feet, shook this massive head. Then it got ready to jump again.

The digital timer interrupted the fight. One of the masked men waiting at the entrance to the arena blew the mysterious whistle. The monster stopped mid-movement, crouching. Falk closed his eyes and took a deep breath. Now I was sure. He was afraid as well.

Money changed hands, the swell of voices grew. At the edge of the fighting pit, next to the transport box, I saw seminude personnel waiting. The next round started way too soon.

This time Falk attacked immediately. He threw himself at the monster, jumped on its back and held tight onto the fur. I held my breath. What the Hel was he doing?

Oh, finishing early, it seemed. His upper arms flexed, the blood flowed faster. He grabbed the muzzle of the beast from behind. The monster bucked. Falk gave the head a violent twist.

The monster went down as if someone had cut the cords.

Lizard Face next to me did not move.

Everyone had fallen silent. The digital timer beeped. The second round had lasted only ten seconds.

A scream rose from the crowd.

For the first time since our arrival, a host interfered. From the tree tops, an artificial finger of light stabbed into the shadows and illuminated a masked gentleman in a suit standing on the other side of the arena. He held a microphone and smiled. "Let's come together to celebrate the victory of man over nature!"

The excitement of the public was transformed to awe. I could feel, almost physically, as the energies changed. My head spun. The silence was creepy. Was this the first time a human fighter had won? My relief was endless. I would get Falk back in one piece!

Or would I?

The host continued, "And this is not the only first we'll have tonight." He made a dramatic gesture towards the bottom of the arena, where Falk was crouching next to the dead thing.

A second box was positioned at the entrance of the ring.

Something was going wrong.

"Our noble hero has promised us five rounds, and five rounds he shall deliver!"

That's not fair, I wanted to shout. He won! What the fuck were they doing? Why were they doing this? And where, for fuck's sake, were the fucking cops?

For the first time I noticed that the men handling the transport box with the next monster were carrying guns. Every one of them was heavily armed. And the looks they shot at the arena were far from friendly. Slowly it dawned on me that this was not at all going the way Falk and Raphael had planned.

A quick glance to Lizard Face – the events had surprised him as well. His face was flushed with excitement. To him, it was only a game, the spice of life, a way to pass time. Maybe he thought of the money he had bet on Falk going five rounds. He seemed to have forgotten that I was there.

Me, on the other hand, I doubted he would get his money. This fight would not end after five rounds – no matter how many monsters Falk killed.

The moment the new box was opened, a pale flash entered the arena and hissed. Six thin legs raced across the uneven floor. A tail with an impressive stinger almost reached the branches of the trees. Arm-long claws cut the air. The yellowish chitin exoskeleton seemed to glow in the spotlight directed at him.

They had brought a fucking scorpion the size of a Shetland pony.

Looking closer, I saw injuries I had not noticed before – bruises that did not come from Falk's first fight. And I recognized his expression. He had never expected to get out of this alive. Something must have gone wrong.

I forced myself to inhale and connect to the surrounding energies. The excitement of the crowd gave me an additional surge. A quick test – no one close to us seemed to know the first thing of magic, and no one was paying me any attention. All eyes were glued to the deadly tragedy playing out below us.

I knew Grete's latest instructions by memory. She had explained where I had gone wrong with the fire spell. I had not yet had time to test her explanation. It did not matter, there was no time for doubt. I kept my eyes closed. Seeing what was happening below me would distract me, scare me. That was one kind of negativity I did not need in my life right now. I put my hand on the tree carefully and –

As the energy left my fingertips, it multiplied and crashed into the home of the wild bees. It felt as if my head was being sucked empty. A giant explosion swept me off my feet. The water in the live wood evaporated, a blinding jet of flame shot into the air. I could hear nothing but swooshing. Burning splinters rained down on me. Once I could see again, I saw dark smoke and an angry cloud of insects attacking everyone around me. Lizard Face was trying to protect his face with clawed hands.

Blood was running into my eyes from a gash in my forehead. I stumbled to my feet and was swept downhill towards the parking lot. While I was running, I collected energy. I had to get past the guards at the entry to the fighting pit. How was I going to do that? No idea. I had plenty of time to think of the details. In fifteen seconds, when I reached the foot of the hill.

I turned towards the arena and one of the seminude people tried to grab me. I ducked under his arm. He got hold of my wig. The pain flashed through my scalp as several strands of hair were ripped out with the pins. I kicked out behind me and my foot connected with something. The guy grunted. I felt him grab my leg. Close combat, really? He must be mad, I weighed at least one hundred pounds less than him. Not fair! I pulled the energy from my core and pushed it into his shoulder with a clumsy hit. Actually I had aimed for his stomach. Good for me, the spell worked just as well. The pure force of the magic pushed him off his feet. His eyes turned upward as if he was trying to look at his own brain and stayed down.

The second guard was nowhere to be seen. Maybe he had rushed off to try and stem the flood of fleeing spectators. I got to my feet, stumbled over a branch and ran to the steel net closing off the arena. There had to be a way to get that thing open!

The box the scorpion had come in stood on a tiny trailer. On top of it was a heavy cable with two buttons. I looked through the net and saw Falk lying on the floor. He used both arms to push against the white belly of his opponent and tried to get his knees up to his chest. His whole body tensed. He pushed the beast off himself and rolled to one side. The stinger hissed through the air and hit the ground where Falk's head had been only a second earlier. Wet ground flew through the air as the monster tore its stinger up again. Down here the air was heavy with the smell of blood and intestines. One of the claws missed Falk by inches as he got up on his feet. I pushed the buttons.

A hidden mechanism above my head awoke. I followed the cable with my eyes and saw a winch pinned to the hills with long metal rods. The net rose in slow motion. My heart beat against my corset. I could not breathe. With jerky movement I got out of my jacket and opened the hooks that held the corset closed in the front. Cold wind caressed my belly. Good thing I was wearing a nice bra.

As soon as the net was high enough, I crawled beneath it into the fighting pit. The scorpion paused, confused, when it saw me stand up. Falk used the opportunity to get out of its reach. He left a wet trail on the leaves. This was not good. The timer beeped in the trees above our heads, declaring the second round over. No one cared. Nobody would come and calm the beast this time. We were on our own.

Chapter 5: Into the woods

The beast turned towards me and made several tiny steps.

My heart skipped a beat. Up close it looked much larger. I needed a defense spell, a plan – anything! But my mind came up empty. The pale exoskeleton seemed to hypnotize me. The giant scorpion pressed its body against the floor and reached high with its tail. It hissed. Somewhere, I had read, if I remembered correctly, that scorpions with stronger poison had tiny claws and big poison glands. If that was true, we were safe – those claws were longer than my lower arm. I retreated towards the exit.

"Get him over to me!", Falk shouted. He was not surprised by my appearance.

What? He wanted me to get closer to the action? That had to be a joke! I looked at him, just a second. His left arm was red with blood and he breathed heavily. Only a few steps and we could be out of here. Panic and chaos were reigning the party around us. No one paid us any attention. No one would try to stop us from leaving. Or try to catch the beast once it had gotten out of here. Damn.

I ran around the scorpion, and it followed me. We got deeper into the arena. The trees had to be somewhere close. I stepped on a branch hidden beneath the leaves and for the fraction of a second feared I might end up on my butt. But I regained my balance and continued my retreat. How far to the wall? A glance over my shoulder and I corrected my course a tiny bit to avoid ending up in a corner. My injured assistant appeared in the corner of my vision. He was limping and pale as a shroud. He held a rock in his right hand and was coming up behind the scorpion.

"Hey, ugly beast!", I shouted to get its attention. I hoped it would not hear Falk creeping closer. Its reach was far greater than that of a human, and I really did not want to bet our lives on the venom being not lethal. The idea of being stabbed with that giant stinger made me sick. And I did not want to be ripped to shreds, either. So I hoped Falk had a plan.

I retreated further and felt rock sliding beneath my feet. The burning tree above our heads made shadows dance in the arena. The air was heavy with tension. Or it might be the sparks dancing around us.

Falk jumped, grabbed the scorpion's tail and pushed it on the floor. He hit it with his rock. Once, twice – opaque fluid squirted through the air. Where droplets hit my skin, a burning sensation started.

The scorpion howled and thrashed.

One of the claws hit Falk before he could get himself out of harm's way. He screamed. A deep gash opened in his shoulder. Blood ran down his chest. The black tank top stuck to his body, wet with blood. He tried to kick the scorpion, but his feet did not connect.

The monster lifted him above its head and started shaking him.

I grabbed another rock and threw myself at them. The tail with the smashed tip raced through the air and hit me like a giant whip. All air was pushed from my lungs and my vision went black. I grabbed one of the legs with my left leg and hit it with the other, but the rock did not make a dent in its exoskeleton.

At least my attack had distracted the scorpion. It dropped Falk, turned in a circle and tried to shake me. Falk disappeared from my vision. I held on for dear life. As long as I stayed up here, close to its body, it could not reach me with its claws. But I did not know how much longer I could hold on.

Something black was moving on the floor. I heard a rustling mixed in with the hissing of the angry beast, then a snapping sound. The scorpion stumbled. One of its legs gave way. I lost my grip and flew through the air. Dry bushes caught my fall.

When I looked up I saw Falk lying under the scorpion's belly. He was holding something long and pointy – a broken branch. The beast reared up over him. I jumped to my feet and raced towards them.

The scorpion hesitated – unsure whom to attack first, who of us was the bigger threat.

Falk got to his knees, lunged forward with all his weight behind the movement, and rammed the branch into the scorpion's body like a spear. He jumped aside just in time for the heavy body to crash into the dead leaves. Then his body disappeared behind the dying arachnid.

I ran around the twitching monster. Its tail was thrashing around, the last movements of a dying giant. A fine rain of bodily fluids and venom was spraying us and burned on my bare skin.

Falk was lying on the ground, trying to breath. I approached and saw that his tank top was in shreds. Long tears ran across his upper body. The black rags clinging to his upper body and the top of his pants were drenched in blood.

"Are you okay?", I asked, even though I knew better, and knelt beside him.

He twisted his face into a smile. "A bit tired. Give me a minute. Say, aren't you cold?"

Too bad we did not have a minute. I looked around nervously. Obviously one of the suit-wearing guys from the parking lot hat remembered the mess in the arena. He came towards us with a determined frown. I bet his employers were not at all happy with the way this evening was going.

I got up and stepped away from Falk to give both of us room to move. The spot light made me feel trapped. If that guy had a weapon … "Is there a problem, Sir?", I asked.

The guy smirked. No sense of humor. We were only a few steps apart from each other when he crouched down, ready to jump.

Something knocked him off his feet. He came down on his belly, moaning. Falk was kneeling next to him, panting. His blood was drenching the floor.

"I could have done that myself", I complained.

Falk ignored me. He turned the other man on his back. The guy was flailing around. Even I could see that he was no real fighter. When Falk hit the front of his neck with his elbow, hard, the movement stopped.

My stomach felt weird. I swallowed.

"Let's get out of here", Falk suggested and staggered to his knees.

"Wait, we have to dress your wounds first", I insisted. I started ripping the dead man's shirt to shreds.

"We don't have time", Falk pleaded.

"Stop squirming!" My hands trembled as I tore the cloth into long strips. I wrapped them around Falk's left arm and upper body. Where the venom had hit his skin, the wounds were red and oozing. I looked down my own body – not much better. We needed water to clean the wounds. But first we had to escape.

The whole action had only taken a few moments. I helped Falk to his feet, ducked under the steel net still half covering the entrance, and waited for him to straighten next to me. His face was a mask of pain. No one was around except for us. We pushed past the empty boxes, reached the path towards the graveled parking lot and ran towards the street. The path was hard to see beneath the trees. The sun had gone down without any of us noticing. We saw luxury cars racing off, spitting gravel at those left behind. Maybe one of the heads I saw ducking into cars belonged to Lizard Face. Hard to tell with all the chaos and darkness. Several men were running through this madness barking orders and curses.

"Quick, this way!" I grabbed Falk's healthy arm and dragged him into the underbrush. We tumbled down a hillside towards the street, crashing through branches. Someone shouted something behind us. More snapping branches. Damn, they must have seen us. A branch whipped into my face. I stumbled and bit my own lip. Behind me I heard Falk's labored breath. We raced onto the tar surface of the street without stopping. Brakes screamed. We froze in the light of an oncoming car – only for a moment. Then the engine roared and the car lurched at us.

Falk was first to react. He dragged me off the street and into the bushes on the other side. We stumbled through a dry ditch and ran on without stopping. Beneath the trees it was so dark that we could only see a step or maybe two ahead of us. Multiple times we crashed into trees that seemed to grow out of nothing. Every inch of my body was hurting, my lungs and thighs were burning after just a few yards. We were running up a steep mountainside, crossing a narrow path and jumping rocks, never stopping.

Finally, we took a break, covering behind a twisted beech tree digging its roots deep into the ground. Time to catch our breaths. I peered around the trunk. Were they still chasing us?

Oh yes, they were. Between the branches and the young leaves, I spied torches stabbing the night. Someone was shouting orders, "Don't let them get away!" How cliché.

Still I intended to thwart their plans. My heart was boxing my ribs from the inside. I turned to Falk, "Are you up for a challenge?"

"I feel like a racing car – after a crash." His eyes seemed to sparkle in the dark. I took the time for a brief energetic scan – not good. Not good at all. On most days Falk was glowing with a satisfied orange which I would have recognized among a million other people. It was almost gone. He could barely keep his feet. And here was I, with my genius escape plan.

"We should go that way", I explained and pointed uphill.

"You're crazy", Falk whispered. "Fleeing up a mountain is the dumbest thing we could do!"

"You're free to go down there again", I answered. "Rumor is they'd love to see you again." Then I got serious. "This is the only way. I know the area a bit. We only have to make it up one third, then there will be plenty of niches and caves for us to hide in."

Falk did not seem convinced. I could understand it, but from what I see we were all out of options.

After a moment he seemed to reach the same conclusion, for he nodded, spit on the dry leaves beneath our feet and started climbing. "Let's go up then."

Every time we looked back we saw lights flickering between the tree. Why the hell could they not simply give up? We crept from tree to tree, hid behind rocks and did our best to remain silent. At least we were harder to spot. My pale upper body was hidden under layers of dirt, and Falk looked the same. We would not reflect the light, that much was sure. Still the situation was not in our favor. Falk had lost too much blood. Once when we had to climb up a set of natural steps made from stone he stumbled, and for a moment I feared he would fall. I could not carry him, that much was sure. He caught himself at the last moment, fingers digging in the dirt, and pulled himself up to me.

At least we were out of harm's way for the moment. Maybe I could call 911 now? I pulled my mobile from my pocket and pushed a button. Greenish light illuminated our faces. The display was cracked and looked as if it had been covered in layers of cobwebs. Then a growing group of dark pixels appeared. I pushed a few buttons, but nothing happened. Either the magical explosion or the fight with the scorpion had destroyed it. So much for the invincibility of Nokia phones. "Damn, the phone's shot."

"Switch it off, they'll see us!", Falk hissed. I complied. He looked scary, to be honest. And I still did not know what had gone wrong back there. Why had the police not interfered? Where was our backup? Plenty of open questions we would need to find answers for. If we survived the night. The way we were going would not take us near other humans for miles. Not the best way to stay alive. It was time for us to get moving again.

The hill got steeper, and we slowed down. The lights were following us without pause. They flickered between the trees. Sometimes I heard shouting. They were itching to get us. I climbed another rock in our path and turned right. Here was a small clearing with corners and niches for hiding – or not. The bushes I had hoped for had been trimmed to within an inch of their lives. Tax money at work. Too bad. There were a few rocks stacked up here and there, but I did not see any way out in case they followed us to this place. The only way on the other side of the clearing was down.

I pointed up. "You go that way. I'll be there in a minute."

Falk obeyed without another word. A bad sign. I looked at his back as he attacked the next climb. Darkness swallowed him almost immediately.

I turned and stepped on the clearing. A tiny scan – even in utter darkness this place was too neat and open to be used as a hiding spot. But the guys chasing us did not know that we knew this. I inhaled – the air smelled of rain. Earth energy vibrated beneath my feet, close to the surface, familiar lines in these mountains. I pulled a minute amount into myself and started stacking pebbles and stones on each other. While the heap grew, I fed it with energy. Now I only needed a spark, so to speak. If I did my job properly, they would send the stones flying as soon as they got closer. It might be enough to lead them on for a while.

I found a branch beneath the trees, energized it between my hands and placed it across the path leading to the clearing. It would be all but impossible to not touch it. Connecting the branch to the pile of stones on an energetic level took me two tries. I was freezing. Time was running out. Finally I was kind of satisfied with the job. I had only seen this kind of trap once before, in a cave beneath another part of the mountains shortly after Samhain. I stepped across my project and started following Falk up the mountainside. He could not have gone far. I looked back and saw the torches close behind me. If we did not find a hiding spot soon, we were screwed. None of us had the energy for a long chase.

The sound coming from the top of the trees changed, and a moment later I felt the first drops of rain at the back of my neck. Soon the paths would grow muddy and harder to climb, and our feet would leave a visible trail. The way we were walking on made a sharp turn to the right and disappeared behind a stone wall. To our left, several huge rocks were leaning against each other, everyone the size of a Korean car. I hesitated. To the right, we would have to climb almost another mile to the top. From there we could choose one of several ways down on the other side. If we made it that far, we would be as good as safe. But Falk did not look as if he would make it. He was waiting for me, leaning against a tree. Although he tried to be quiet, his breath seemed to scream in my ears. His face was white and covered in sweat. I looked at him and saw him swaying as he closed his eyes. It was decided.

I pushed him to the left, between the rocks. He stumbled over a thick tree root and grabbed a piece of rock to keep his feet. Right in front of him there was a dark nothing. My arm shot out to keep him from falling. A deep crack cut through the mountains. The other side was hardly visible. My heart skipped a beat.

I poked him and pointed at a gap under an overhanging rock. "Quick, this way!" As soon as he had disappeared in the dark, I got down on all four and followed him.

The cave grew bigger after the entry. Still it was only four feet high. Dry leaves covered the ground. People on the path would not be able to spot us. Or that was what I hoped. A quick glance showed neither beer bottles nor condoms lying around – the cave seemed to be a secret, with not even teenagers aware of its existence. Or maybe they were too lazy to climb this far for a bit of loneliness. Well, I did not care. I prayed to the gods that the people chasing us would walk right past. We were all out of superpowers.

I stretched out on the ground at the back of the cave, with my shoulders propped against the cold wall. A ledge was poking me. "Come here!" I pulled Falk against me. He moaned and ended up flat on his back, his head resting in my lap.

For a long time we stayed quiet, listening. The rain drowned out all sounds of the night. Even with someone passing right in front of the cave, we would not have heard them. The thought made me nervous. On the other hand they would not hear us, either. "How are your injuries?", I whispered.

"Still there", he answered. "Put your hand in my left pocket."

I did as he had told me. My fingers closed around a tiny tube with a longish plastic lid. I switched on the display of my phone for a moment to read the label. Superglue? What in hell did we need that for?

Falk seemed to read my mind. "It will help stop the bleeding."

"Are you mad? I am not going to glue you together like a broken mug!"

"Hush!" He listened into the darkness. "Chemically speaking, this is the same stuff as the glue used in the OR."

"Are you sure?"

"I've used this before when I got the short end of the bargain."

Oh, then it was alright. Really, obviously, after all it had worked in the past, and he had survived.

"Just use it on the deep cuts", he instructed, "the scratches will heal on their own."

My mouth went dry. We crawled around inside our care, with the phone display illuminating the bloody scene for fractions of seconds, while I treated Falk's upper body and two of the injuries in his upper arm with the glue. I squeezed a few drops into each wound and pressed it close tightly, as he had told me. This was not the most sterile workplace I could imagine, but what could I do?

With one last moan Falk rolled over on his back and put his head on my thigh. "I'll sleep over it and wake up as good as new."

Me, I was not as sure about the whole thing. Carefully I screwed the lid back on the tube. Outside the rain kept falling. I crept to the front of the cave and washed the scorpion venom off my bare skin. Carefully I lifted my head over the rocks to look out for persecutors, but they were nowhere to be seen. The rain and the darkness had masked our escape sufficiently, it seemed. Everything was black, and I was not sure the quiet had a calming effect. But instead of worrying, I drenched a few of my rags in a puddle and crawled back to Falk to clean him off as well.

Then there was nothing more to do. We sat in a tiny bubble in a vast university, did not speak, and waited for what would inevitably happen. Sometimes I dozed off for a few moments. My backside was wet, as was the ground I was sitting on, and Falk's hot cheek was burning through my torn pants.

After an eternity he spoke, and his voice mixed with the falling droplets. I bent over him to hear what he was saying. My back, cold and cramping, creamed protest. "Back there, standing in the ring, I really thought it would be over. Could have known that you would not let me escape like that." He breathed in. "Thank you."

"Don't mention it", I answered meekly and buried my fingers in his dark hair. "Get some rest."

"If my parents knew this … well, they always expected it. They would be surprised I'm still alive."

Of course I had to know. "Why did you agree to this?" He really needed a hairdresser appointment.

"Maybe I thought I could end everything in a good way, kind of. Beat fate. Something like that."

"Do you know another way to beat fate?", I boxed his shoulder gently and felt him wince. "Stay out of trouble and die of old age!"

"And how likely is that?"

To that, I had nothing to say. Why did he not at least try? Damn, how quickly I had gotten used to him … if something happened to him now – I did not know what I would do then. Saying that I would miss him was an understatement. I decided not to think about the consequences of the things going on in my mind.

"My grandfather was a really careful guy. He had a ship on the river, his very own. His most dangerous hobby was the toy train in the basement. He did not drink, did not travel to exotic places and did not mingle with other people. On his way to the ship, one day, he was hit by a drunk kid in a car and died." He shifted his weight and inhaled through his teeth. "If he didn't make it, how could I?"

No, I would not let him get away this easily. Once we were home I would find a way to kick this curse's ass. Just had to take a closer look at it. I leaned my head against the rock and closed my eyes.

And somehow I must have fallen asleep, for the next time I opened my eyes dawn was creeping up on us. The rain had lost interest, and the downpour had shrunk back to a soft murmur on the leaves. The treetops were swaying gently above our heads. And someone was nearby.

Falk had heard it as well. He was lying completely still, but I knew he was awake. Then he got up, inch by inch. His face twisted with pain, but he did not make a sound.

A branch snapped.

My thoughts tumbled over each other. How likely was it that they had chased us down with a magic tracker? The connection between Falk and me was not exactly secret. Maybe they knew exactly whom they were looking for. In this case I would give our location away by collecting energy. On the other hand – people with this kind of talent were not exactly growing on trees. And I could not sit and do nothing! This was the best way to get caught. Somehow I did not think that these people would sit us down for a stern talk and then let us go. If they had not hurt Falk this badly, we would have been gone last night. Instead we had curled up and hoped that the problem would simply go away. Nothing wrong with wishing, right?

Falk turned to face me and smiled. He smelled as if he needed a shower, wood mixed with sweat, and he was pale as death. The places where the venom had touched his skin were red and inflamed. Tiny drops of sweat stood on his forehead, although the night had been cold. Minuscule movement attracted my attention – a beetle was crawling over his shoulder. I leaned forward and brushed the insect aside.

His smile turned sad. Our future did not look too bright right now. I held my breath as he extended his hand to touch my face, slowly. At the last moment he made a fist. It raced at my face like a comet, and then the world turned black.

Chapter 6: To serve and protect

The clock on the wall was ticking away. I sat on my moss-green visitor's chair, stiff as a wand, tearing a paper tissue apart. My left cheekbone pulsed. I knew it was shining in all colors of the rainbow, but I had been too angry to hide it with either makeup or magic.

When I had regained consciousness in the woods, Falk had been gone. The rain had stopped, and there had been no trace of our persecutors – except for the trails left by the cars in the mud to either side of the street cutting through the hills. Although I looked terrible – mud-caked, only half dressed and covered in bruises and scratches – some business suit stopped his snow-white BMW and took me into town. Of course he made me sit on a blanket he got from his trunk. Without a word he dropped me in front of the police station. Which was where I was sitting now, waiting for Raphael.

At first the nice guy at the front desk had tried to persuade me to talk to a female officer. I was not quite sure what he expected … okay, that was a lie. I knew pretty well what he thought had happened, but I did not have time for people I could not shout at. Hence I had insisted on seeing Raphael. He was responsible for the mess we were in.

I was going through the story in my mind once more when the door behind me opened. I turned my head and gritted my teeth. Dry mud rained from my hair onto the linoleum. Finally. "Where. Have. You. Been?" My voice was dangerously calm.

I did not know whether anyone had told Raphael about the physical condition I was in. His face did not betray any emotion as he looked at me. Still he kept a safe distance.
"Helena, we –"

100

"Don't start. You've botched it. What happened?"
Every word came out slightly louder than the one before.

He went over to a narrow wardrobe and pulled out an old sweater. "Here, put this on. I assume you went there?"

"Yeah, and I didn't see any of your people around. Where were they?" I all but screamed the last sentence. Falk was gone, probably in the hands of people who would not shy away from murder. He might be dead already. And the police, for whom he had taken a beating, had left him hanging. To protect and serve, my ass.

Raphael gave my chair a wide berth. He treated me like a dangerous animal. With a sigh he sat down at his desk and started pushing a thin paper file from one side to the other and back. "Something must have given him away. They found the GPS tracker sewn into his clothes, right at the beginning. They were still at their initial location in Bonn. His surveillance detail was late, we could not identify the arena."

Yeah, I knew. "So you're saying someone ratted him out?" I sounded like someone in a cheap movie.

He shook his head. "I don't know."

"And what are we going to do now? Are you going to help me get Falk back?" I hated that my voice sounded almost as if I was begging. Still I could not stop myself. They had to.

"We will do our best to find your assistant. After all he is our only witness." Raphael looked me in the eye. "Except for you, of course."

"As you can guess, I was hit on the head pretty badly", I lied without missing a beat. "It may be a while before my memory returns. Falk would make a much better witness, don't you think so?" If he thought I was going to help them …

Raphael watched me closely. "I guess you made some shady deal to get to the place. And as witnesses go, your reputation isn't the best to begin with."

That should have stung, but it was not an insult – it was a fact. Most judges and lawyers did not like to have witches and magicians on the witness stand, even without made-up memory loss. Probably afraid of being hexed.

Raphael coughed. "Don't worry, you'll get your assistant back."

"Unless you mess up again. Like you did yesterday."

We looked at each other for a moment, none of us willing to back down. Look at it whichever way you wanted, Raphael's team had fucked up on a grand scale. If it had not been for them, I could get mad about stinking gym wear in my hallway right now.

"Fine", he finally switched topics, "tell me whatever it is you remember."

"The memory loss …", I started.

"Save it."

Ah well. "We were in the woods, somewhere behind the monastery. Plenty of fine folks, like the opera."

He made me point out the location on a map, then asked, "Did you recognize anyone?"

I thought about that. Of course I had not wasted much time on my surroundings. And Sterling – I would go after him myself. We had worked together for years. He owed me an explanation. So I shook my head. "I did not recognize anyone except for the people I came with."

"Would those people be willing to talk to us?"

"I don't know."

"Not really upstanding citizens, I guess." Raphael took some notes before he returned all his attention to me. "And what happened next?"

I gave him an abbreviated version of the events – up to the moment where were hid in the cave on the other side of the street, up in the mountains. Raphael did not say a word, instead he listened and scribbled on his notepad.

Once I was done talking, he continued writing for a moment and then leaned back. "The woman you told me about was found this morning. At the back of a highway parking lot, two towns south of here. Do you remember what she fought against?"

"A choo- tsuchigumo, it was."

"Could you repeat that?"

"A tsuchigumo". The second time the word came way easier. "A being from Japanese folklore", I explained. "Basically a mix of human and spider."

Raphael shuddered. "I hope it did not lay eggs in her body."

That was an image I did not need in my mind right now. I shook it off, a physical effort, and more mood rained down on the ground. "Can I go now? I'm tired."

"Come on, I'll take you home." Raphael pushed his chair back.

"Don't bother, I'll grab a cab."

"You don't have any money on you."

"Then I'll take the subway. The station is right around the corner."

"I can't let you fare-dodge, you know that." He stood and walked towards the door. "No arguing – it's the least I can do for you right now."

We did not speak as we walked down into the garage where rows of police cars were waiting. I ignored the stares of the officers we passed in the hallway. Most people who looked the way I did right now probably did not come to the police station voluntarily, bruised and dragged. At least I did not have to face them with my boobs out in the open anymore.

"Where's your Renault?", I asked as we stopped so Raphael could unlock a black Toyota.

"That's my private car. This one's for official rides."

"Got a towel I could put on the seat?"

"Don't worry. Get in already."

So they did not clean their cars themselves. I dropped into the seat, fastened my belt and hunkered down as low as was possible.

The tires screamed when Raphael accelerated the car and we shot out onto the street. Someone honked behind us. I was pressed against the passenger door as we whooshed around a corner. It took him not even a minute to cross the river. Neither of us spoke a word. I was busy gripping the upholstery with both hands. In front of a traffic light, we stopped abruptly. As we stood waiting, I realized for the first time in hours that I was hungry. Raphael pushed down on the gas pedal again when the light turned green, and we entered the tunnel. He braked shortly in front of the speed cameras, and soon we were out in the open again.

"Turn right", I instructed him at the next crossing.

"Why?"

"I need a new phone." And I had to get my SIM card again – after all it was my official number. That was a problem I would have to solve without Raphael's help, unless I wanted to anger the shapeshifters.

With his police Id behind the windshield it was no problem for Raphael to park his car somewhere on the main street, right in front of the next phone shop. Still it took me a while and a visit to two more shops before one salesman handed me a phone that was "of age older than Noah's Flood", as he explained. He hesitated to take money for it. But I flat out refused his smartphone offers, they were too expensive and sensitive for my lifestyle.

"You need SIM?", he asked, putting the ancient device into a plain white bag.

"No, thanks", I refused, took the bag and left the shop. I was glad that the hood of Raphael's sweatshirt was hiding my injuries. Without another word we returned to the car and drove to my place.

He parked directly across from my house. His driving style had made me slightly nauseous. "Should I come inside?", he asked, looking at me.

"No, I'm fine." I unfastened the seatbelt and got out of the car. Then I waited at the curb until he had turned his car around and disappeared down the hill. Maybe he would go back to the station, or to the next crime scene. I did not care.

The garden gnomes on my front lawn had no idea what had happened since I left yesterday. Their hats glinted in the sunlight. The sign put between them was tilted slightly. I stopped and pushed it back upright with the tip of my foot. The front door, only a few feet away, seemed like an insurmountable obstacle. Once I opened it and did not fall over the gym bag, I could not tell myself that everything had only been a nightmare.

If Strega had missed me, it did not show. I found her on the sofa, enjoying the sunlight. Her body formed a fluffy circle of content. She did not look as if she was starving. And Maria was busy in the office, as was the case on most days. I was not sure whether I wanted to see her right now. She must be wondering where we were anyway. Maybe if I crept up the stairs really quietly …

"There you are! I've been worrying!"

Yeah, no luck. Too bad. I turned around, a lopsided smile nailed to my face. "Took a bit longer than expected."

"And you lost your wig on the way, I see. Where's Falk?"

I looked out of the window. Last night's rain had washed away the colors from the ribbons tied to my apple tree. They hung in the mild spring air like limb worms. The longest touched the daffodils growing around the stem.

"Helena? Is everything alright?"

Breath. Just breathe. Don't cry. I heard the wheels of her wheelchair behind me and clenched my fists tightly. "There's been trouble", I said with an even voice. Then I bent down and held my hand out for Strega for examination. "Falk has disappeared."

The silence hovered about us as the reality settled in. Strega pushed her head against my fingers.

"I'm sorry", Maria said quietly.

I nodded. Then I changed the topic. "Thanks for taking care of Strega."

"I bet she wouldn't have died if she had had to wait for a few more hours. She is getting a little soft around the middle."

"Still, thank you." I swallowed. "I think I should get rid of the mud and get dressed. Anything I have to take care of?"

Maria shook her head. "I sent our a few bills, and two late notices. No new requests."

And for once I was grateful that work was slow. "Take the day off, will you. I'll try to get some sleep."

She looked at me, unsure whether she could really leave me alone. Then she nodded. "I'll file a few more papers, then I'm out of here. And …" She hesitated. "If you don't mind, I'll light a candle for Falk."

"That would be nice", I replied. Then I turned, walked around her wheelchair and climbed up the stairs to my bedroom.

The bed had not been made, and a wet spot had formed under the window. On the right a pair of dirty black socks was lying on the floor. I stared at them for a long time, then turned on my heel and marched into the bathroom.

More dried mud rained from my clothing when I peeled them off my body. My boots looked terrible, but it might be possible to save them with a brush, a bit of warm water and lots of oil. Or at least I hoped so. The pants had collected even more tears, I would probably not wear it anymore. Raphael's sweatshirt ended up on the floor. I hesitated with the hand on the faucet. Shower or bath? Immersing myself in hot water sounded promising – getting away from everything – forget reality for a while. I doubted, however, that the bath would result in a relaxing day. So I got in the shower an scrubbed myself thoroughly, then grabbed my morning gown and wrapped myself. Today the wild colors did not lift my spirits.

The bed had not changed since I had entered the bathroom. I bet the pillows still smelled of him.

I went down into the living room and turned the sofa into a bed with help of a few throw pillows and a blanket. Strega came running and hopped on the sofa before I had a chance to get into bed. I moved as close to her as I dared, until I could feel her purring against my belly. I was dead tired. Through the closed lids I saw the sun like an orange

108

veil in front of the window. My thoughts started dancing in circles. Where was Falk right now? Had they hurt him? Was he even still alive?

No, I interrupted myself, don't even think about it. Get your shit together! I turned around and buried my head in the pillows. Strega, annoyed by my movement, jumped off the sofa and disappeared from the room. Suddenly I felt terribly alone.

After a while I sat up again. I could not sleep anyway. Maybe I should go out running? But what if someone called while I was out?

I could take my new phone. But wait, Lizard Face still had my SIM card. And – why should they call me? Don't play dumber than you are. This was no kidnapping or blackmail. They were just trying to get rid of witnesses.

And what if they knew where to find me? My heart skipped a beat. My home was safe, I had made sure of that when I moved in, but I could not really take a circle of protection with me into the woods. Too much trouble. And no spell in the world would keep me from getting shot. Not even I was that good. So running was off the table.

But I could not stay seated here without doing anything – just wait for the bad news – not my cup of tea.

A rubber mouse was lying in front of the sofa, one of Strega's neglected toys. I threw it into the hallway, heard it squeak and then a thump as Strega jumped off the kitchen table, starting a paper avalanche. Time to get moving.

The altar in my bedroom had started to collect dust. Since the weather allowed it, I had been doing my rituals outside in the garden, protected from the neighbors' curiosity by a tall hedge. I blew on the table twice, raising dust from the green tablecloth, and pushed my tools around until everything looked right. By now I had gotten attached to the Ereschkigal statue in the middle. Her feet were covered in wax drops from all the candles I had burned for her since last November.

No, I could not work like this. Carefully I cleaned everything away and shook out the green cloth. With a wet rag I cleaned the round table, dried the wooden surface carefully and spread the cover over it once more. Then I cleaned my tools – chalice, athame, wand and the silvery piece of charcoal representing the element of Earth for me. The rest of my paraphernalia changed from time to time, but this was a gift from a client I had gotten used to a long time ago. It left a storm grey smudge on the rag when I cleaned it.

I put a thick white candle in the middle of the table, Ereschkigal next to it. The statue was wearing a tiny lion mask made from leather. My incense of choice was juniper, dried, on a sieve over a tiny candle. The heavy smell spread through the room in a matter of seconds. I filled the glass chalice with tap water. Then I took the tarot cards from the shelf. I needed answers.

Most of all I needed something to represent Falk. I looked around. He had been living here for three months, but the amount of personal items he had amassed here was tiny. I ended up taking his used razor and wrapping a piece of red thread around the handle to symbolize our connection. I pressed the blades against the ring finger of my left hand until I saw blood. I let it drop onto the thread. Slowly my inner self calmed down. I felt the energy of past rituals rising. In these moments my bedroom was a special place.

110

I took my time drawing a circle to form a safe place between the worlds and sat down on a pillow in the west. In my mind I pictured a glass of clouded water. I inhaled deeply, again and again, until the fluid had cleared and all the debris had sunk to the ground. Then I connected to Heaven and Earth and started listening.

The reflections in the water-filled chalice did not yield any results, despite the smoke. I tried looking at it without seeing, without concentrating, and saw shadows moving, but no details. Maybe it was because my thoughts kept wandering – back to the other side of the river, to our tiny cave in the mountains. Every time I thought I was at peace for a moment, worry fluttered inside my chest and thwarted my attempts at seeing new information. In the end I gave up and grabbed my tarot cards. My fingers brushed against the chalice, but I caught it before it poured water over the altar.

Many witches have an almost ridiculous love for tarot decks. There are hundreds of varieties – Renaissance Tarot, Egyptian Tarot, Gothic Tarot, Elf Tarot. Vampire Tarot. Garden Gnome Tarot. Wise Women Tarot. During my studies I had seen dozens, in class for demonstrations as well as in the hands of my fellow students. They had wasted hours comparing the symbols of their decks and fawning over the pictures.

My mother had given me a Rider Waite Tarot for my thirteenth birthday – a classic. The cards were worn and dented. I had not taken much when I ran away from home, but these cards had been in my backpack. They had seen almost as much of the world as I had.

Instead of spreading the cards, face down, on a piece of cloth, I mixed them with my hands. Way quicker. Then I drew the first card and put it on the floor in front of me. The next three formed a triangle around it. Then I started turning them around to look at the message.

The tower – deep breath. I felt something opening up in my chest. The image was scary: Lightning tearing into an ancient building, people falling through the air. These people held the secret to the card that gave me hope. Everyone depicted on this card was still alive. It was not too late for Falk after all.

Next I uncovered "Seven Rods". Easy to understand: One against everyone else. So I would have to do everything myself. I caressed the worn edges of the card. This was a situation I knew all too well.

The next card was not as easy to read. Eight cups – that could be a voyage with an unknown outcome, or a separation. Maybe the last card would tell me more. I held out my hand and hesitated.

A crowned woman on a throne, holding a blade. The Queen of swords. What was the name my teacher had given her? Devil's Assassin. The one woman everyone had to watch out for. She could be a tough opponent or a priceless ally.

My tarot cards had never let me down. Once again they delivered all the answers – in a foreign language I would only be able to decipher when it was too late. Still it calmed me to see the future. I turned the cards around, pushed them in between the others, and put them on the altar. Then I prayed.

Ereschkigal rarely replied when I spoke to her, but I always felt her presence. Today she was watching me through the eyes of the statue, hidden behind a lion's mask, and remained silent. Her mouth seemed to move, but that might be an illusion caused by the smoke. I sniffed the candle flame out with my fingers. There would be no more visions today. I would have to take action in the real world.

Chapter 7: Identification

The limousine raced down the street under the bridge and squealed to a stop inches in front of a pillar. The car doors slammed, and between the shadows I saw people appear. They were talking and laughing. Lizard Face and his companions had arrived. Finally

For more than one hour I had been waiting between the parked cars, waiting for the gang. I needed more information. If I was about to travel – and I hoped that the tarot cards had shown travel instead of separation – I had to learn all there was to know. Or find out who was responsible for this madness. That might be the one who had Falk.

Of course I was working based on guesses. I had not seen them take him captive. I did not even know for a fact whether the people who had chased us were the guys working for the illegal fighting circle. But let us be realistic – who else should be interested in catching us? Well, not me, but Falk had been in contact with the organizers. He possibly knew enough to blow all their covers. They were playing it safe, I assumed. That was why they could not let him get away. Maybe they had killed him then and there, at least that would put an end to his suffering. I was not sure what I was praying for. Theoe guys had not looked too nice.

Be that as it may, in the end I preferred the theory that Falk was still alive … and unharmed, if possible. This gave me the option to do something. Which was why I was here.

I waited until the men were close, took a deep breath and stepped out from between the cars.

They stopped, surprised. Only for a moment, but it was enough time for me to close the distance between us. My heart was racing. By the time they recovered from their surprise, I had their leader by the neck.

He made a half-hearted attempt to swat me away like an annoying fly.

Sparks flew from my fingertips. More than I had planned. Ouch. His hoodie and eyebrows started smoldering.

"Take a step back, or he will go up in flames!", I shouted at the other men. My voice held more determination than I felt. I could sense the energy quiver inside of me, flaring with anger. It would be too bad if I turned us into human torches by accident.

The men seemed to think the same, because they gave us room. "What do you want?", asked Lizard Face. His voice was calm, but up close I could see his pupils change shape. I had learned that this sometimes happened to shapeshifters when they were nervous. Or maybe he was preparing to tear me to pieces. I knew he was fighting dirty. With a push of my thoughts I sent another burst of sparks at his face. Several of his scales curled up in the heat and started to crack. And Lizard Face, even though he was half a head taller than I was, held still.

"Can we talk like normal people?", I asked, sounding calmer than I felt.

"Sure." He gave the tiniest hint of a nod.

I hoped my face did not betray my relief. "And your two friends will remain peaceful?"

"Of course." His throat twitched. Lizard Face's breath smelled of cumin and onions. I guessed he had had shawarma for lunch. You could get it at any corner around here, and they tasted fantastic.

"First, I need my SIM card back", I whispered in his ear. To support my request I made the air at the edge of his vision flicker.

He nodded to Vulture. That one pushed his hand into his pocket, very slowly, pulled a tiny piece of plastic out of it and held it high so I could see it.

"Put it on the transporter over there." I waited until he had followed my instructions. Then I let go of Lizard Face and took two steps back. It would be stupid to stay close to him after humiliating him in front of his friends. "Last night you were gone pretty quickly."

No sign of shame. Running away was in, it seemed. "We had an appointment."

"I am not complaining. You were not the only ones leaving dust trails." I walked around the men, took my SIM card from the car and put it in my new phone. With quick glances I made sure that the shapeshifters stayed where they could not grab me. When I pushed the button at the top of the phone, an old-fashioned animation moved across the display. I felt relief that did not at all match my distrust against modern technology. And the sensation did not last, for I had neither messages nor calls waiting for me.

Lizard Face watched me closely. He was clever enough to keep his distance. "Seems you got away as well."

"Not thanks to you. And they caught my assistant."

"The giant scorpion?", one of the other men asked. He sounded as if the beast had impressed him. I itched to hit him.

Instead I took a deep breath. "No, the guys. And you will tell me where I can find them."

Lizard Face shook his head. "Sorry, Darling, that won't work. No one knows who organizes these things."

"And how did you get that invitation?", I asked. "That went pretty quick."

"They have their contact channels. Same as we do."

"Then tell me who I have to talk to."

"No chance. Not even if you could turn piss into gold." He saw anger flare up in my eyes and held up his hands. "Chica, I am sorry that they got your guy. But if they learn I am giving away their information, I'm done. I would never survive that."

Good to know that I was not the only one to be afraid of them. But this did not help me one little bit. "Is there anything you can tell me?"

"Did you get a closer look at the boxes?"

"The boxes?"

"The ones they kept the beasts in."

I shook my head.

"I bet they were covered in customs stickers." He looked at me as if I was supposed to have some genius idea. But my mind remained dark.

"Dutch custom stickers", he added, as if that should tell me something.

I tilted my head and waited. Was there anything else?

"Don't act more stupid than you are!" Lizard Face spat on the floor. "Almost all beasts and magic pets come here via Amsterdam."

Amsterdam? "How do you know?"

He grinned. "I know someone. He helps us every now and again if we have to buy … herbs. He helps us find skippers who can be trusted with precious … herbs. Sometimes we talk over drinks."

"Can you tell me what he's called?"

"No way." He turned to his friends. "I knew the chick was crazy. No, Darling, and I won't call him for you, either. But it should not be too hard to find out who gets his beasts that way."

He might be right. I felt something vibrate in my pocket and dug for my mobile. The standard ringtone sounded weird, and I did not know the number on the display, either. I pushed the green button. "Yes?"

"Helena?"

"What a surprise!", I joked. "How did you know I was in Riverton?"

Either he did not get my sense of humor, or he was running out of patience. "Can you come to my office once more?"

"I'll be there in twenty minutes."

"Fine, see you." He hung up on me.

I looked at the men and shrugged. "Sorry, but I'll have to leave. Important date, you know."

The BMW took me to the police station in a few minutes. I took the narrow roads on the other side of the river and pushed past parking cars blocking narrow roads, tiny shops in aging buildings. This way I avoided work day traffic closing most streets in Riverton from dawn till dusk. Farther south, getting closer to the Telcom headquarters, the streets grew wider and smoother, grew more lanes, and I accelerated. Few minutes behind the roundabout the police station sat waiting for me. I parked in front of huge windows, hung my helmet from the handle and pushed the button next to the door.

The reception was manned by a different officer this time. And he had been expecting my arrival. As soon as I had stated my reason for coming, he called a female officer who brought be to the basement, where Raphael was waiting. We walked in silence, passing tightly locked doors, beneath flickering neon lights and towards a broad set of double doors with tiny thick wondows set at eye level. Behind I could see several men and women in white overalls busy examining last night's evidence. I felt the first tendrils of magic, like coming home.

The officer who had brought me here made no effort to open the doors. "The procedures beyond these doors are strictly confidential." She pushed a button, and I heard a buzz. One of the white shapes straightened and came to us. I recognized Raphael's short blond hair and his confident gait. This was his home turf. He smiled, briefly, when he saw me, and opened the door. "Helena, that was fast."

119

"I thought we had important stuff to take care of." I craned my neck to see past him. "Is that the crate they used to transport the scorpion?"

"We've just finished the scan for energies."

"Found anything?"

He shook his head, and his mouth twisted. "You know I cannot talk to you about an ongoing investigation."

Bullshit. "You could ask me to assist you."

"We have our experts."

"I trust my own expertise more than your experts."

"Really?" He crossed his arms in front of his chest. "Anything you can tell us that I do not know already?"

I closed my eyes and cocked my head as if I was listening to something. "I know things I shouldn't know. For example, that the crates went through customs in Amsterdam."

When I opened my eyes again, Raphael's smile was gone. "You saw the crates in the woods", he guessed.

"We were busy running for our lives", I replied. "Do you really think I would waste time reading customs stickers?"

"Still I can't let you see the evidence. Come up to my office, I want to show you a few things."

"Will you tell me what you found, at least?"

He looked back over his shoulder. Between the people I could see Patrick bending over a microscope. Then Raphael turned back to me, put a hand on my shoulder and directed me away from the doors.

Back up the stairs we went, following another narrow hallway to his office. The wall to our left consisted of floor-to-ceiling windows offering a nice view of a green patio. I had never imagined a police station to be this – homey. Well, why shouldn't they have it comfortable= After all they were risking their lives for us. I walked through the door Raphael held open for me and sat down on the chair I had left a few hours earlier. I did not feel as if I had achieved anything worth mentioning in the meantime.

"We have collected the profiles of several suspects." Raphael sat down on the other side of the desk. "I would like you to go through them and tell me whether you recognize anyone." He put a heavy file down in front of me and opened the first page.

I leafed through the profiles and looked at every one carefully. Most pictures looked like proper mugshots. A few more appeared to be application pictures. I did not see anyone I knew. Finally I pointed at the picture of a young man with worn army jacket and Mohawk haircut. "I think I've seen him. And his buddy from the other page."

Raphael brushed his fingers through his short hair. He seemed disappointed. "No one else?"

I shook my head.

"Do you remember anyone else? Maybe you could work with one of our artist and –"

"You've got to be kidding me."

My outburst seemed to surprise him. "It might be important to –"

"My assistant has been abducted by violent criminals, and you expect me to sit with one of your Bob Ross guys and watch him paint birds?" I pushed my chair back and watched him defiantly. "If that is all you got, I'm out of here."

He tried to keep his patience with me, I could see that. "I understand that you are upset."

"Obviously you don't." The anger rose from my belly like a snake in the spring sun.

"Would you be willing to testify in court?"

I grabbed my backpack and turned to the door. "I think we're done."

He bent over his desk to grab my arm. "Wait – ouch!" He pulled his hand back and looked at his fingers, searching for burns.

I had not done it on purpose – the defense spell had gotten away from me, so to speak. This had not happened in a long time. I had to be more agitated than I had thought. Not a good sign. I had to do something before I lost my mind.

"Attacking an official with magic is a severe crime." He tried to smile to take the threat out of his words, but it did not reach his eyes.

"Grab me again and I'll give you reason to complain." I took a step back, for I did not trust myself.

He saw it on my face and decided that sitting back down was the best he could do. "It's okay. Let's just talk."

I had to make a decision – either I walked out the door now, with all consequences, or I talked to him. There was something about Raphael that pushed all my buttons. On the other hand I did not want to cut my connection to the police and the information they might turn up. I wanted to rage, grab him by the throat and shake what little he knew from his head, run out there and save Falk with my own bare hands … and I did not even know where he was. So I swallowed my racing heart back into my chest and sat down. "Show me what you've got."

"Say again?"

"I want to know what you know."

Raphael probably hated that I was their only connection to the whole case. He tried to stay calm. "I can't do that."

"Why not?"

"You're our witness. We can'T use you as a witness and as an expert both."

"Then show me the stuff as a witness. It might help my memory." Of course I was bluffing.

He sighed and grabbed something from a drawer. "Do you always get your way?"

"Tends to happen. I am the best after all." I made a face and bent over the tiny plastic bag he had put on the table. "What is that?"

"Fecal matter."

"Yuck. What are they good for?"

"We took several samples from the box. Looks as if it has been used before to transport cryptids. Some samples are older than others."

"And what are they doing in your desk? Are you trying to grow tomatoes?"

"I've got an appointment to talk to an expert at university to learn more about the species we have identified. Do you want to come along?"

That was more than I had expected. I nodded. Finally there was something I could do. My heart did a little joyful jig.

"I expect you to tell the professor everything about the creatures you have seen and how they behaved."

I nodded again. If he wanted to, I would reenact the fights for him. Of course I knew that I had gotten no step closer to Falk. But I had something to keep myself busy, did not have to sit around any longer waiting for his dead body to be found near the river.

My goodness, I really did not expect to get him back alive. The realization landed on my stomach like a block of ice. Tears welled up in my eyes. Don't cry! I gritted my teeth and blinked in rapid succession until I was sure I would not embarrass myself. When I spoke my voice sounded almost normal again. "Can we go already?"

I followed Raphael's car with my bike. The Institute of Cryptozoology, so much I had been told, was located in the woods near where I lived. I had even passed it a time or three – an ivy-choked estate in the middle of an old-fashioned park landscape surrounded by absurdly high electric fences to keep out unwanted guests. Or maybe, I reconsidered, the fences were meant to keep unassuming visitors to be eaten by the nightmares roaming the park. There was no shield, no sign at all to warn passers-by of the things happening behind the fences. On my previous walks I had not seen any way to enter the park. You could say that I was quite a nosey witch.

We neared the iron gate and stopped in the driveway. Gravel crunched beneath my tires. The wind whispered in the branches of the chestnut trees. Through the rear window of Raphael's car I saw him holding a phone up to his ear, talking. And as if moved by ghosts, the gate opened to let us pass. None of my magic senses tingled. Old-fashioned electricity, it seemed. I followed the car carefully, not faster than at walking pace, to the front door. We parked in front of a sweeping staircase. While Raphael unbuckled his seatbelt and got out of the car, I took off my helmet and shook out my hair. If this were an advertisement, my brown locks would bounce around merrily. Instead some stubborn strands had caught under the collar of my jacket. For a second I considered a short haircut.

An older gentleman in a worn, previously white laboratory coat came down the stairs and welcomed us with a friendly smile. His hair used to be black, I could see, and had retreated from the top of his head, which looked like a friendly egg. He shook Raphael's hand and said, "What an unpleasant chain of events." Then he turned to me, "Miss Willow. It pains me to meet you under these circumstances."

I smiled and mumbled greetings. No one had called me "Miss" in quite a while. After a moment I realized something else: The guy had heard of me before. The only place where I had ever encountered his name was a heavy tome on cryptozoology – Professor Eckard Whiteberg, internationally renowned luminary on Mediterranean cryptids of the present. If there was one person in the world who could help us identify the beasts I had seen, it was him. The thought made me nervous and relieved at the same time.

"We had best talk in my office. There you can explain all the details to me. I guess this is confidential?"

Raphael nodded.

Professor Whiteberg led us through the ground floor, past a series of white doors with windows at eye level. From the outside the institute might look like a grand estate of old nobility, on the inside everything had been redesigned for practicality. The floor was black stone with tiny white spots, the walls – added later, I would have bet my pentagram on that – white and bare. It looked like every university building I had ever entered. And as in all university buildings I had entered, people had scribbled on the walls. Students seemed to have an ingrained urge to leave a piece of themselves – either in science or in the shape of vandalism. The professor walked with quick, impatient steps and I had to hurry to keep up with him. His coat fanned out behind him like a flag. While walking I craned my neck to see what happened in the rooms we passed, but I saw nothing but more white coats working with their backs to the doors. Maybe they kept the monsters in the basement?

The men realized I was falling behind. Raphael rolled his eyes. The professor only smiled. "Do you have an interest in cryptozoology?"

"A little bit", I admitted. "I never had the opportunity to take courses as a student, I'm afraid." And right now I

126

wanted to know everything about who – or what – was trying to kill my assistant.

Assistant? Nothing more? Be honest with yourself, woman.

I swallowed and chased the thought with a shake of my head. Later there would be more than enough time to sort these pesky feelings out.

"Would you like a tour?", the professor offered.

"Thanks, maybe another day." At the moment I preferred to get right to the center of the problem.

The professor's office was at the end of the hallway, behind a bent. Through the window I saw a bunch of piglets playing in the mud.

"Are those were-pigs?", I asked.

"We use them as food", the professor explained. He sat down behind a narrow desk buried under papers. The gleaming chrome frame holding up the files seemed to bend under the load. I spotted a few white plastic trays, but no order. Seemed I was not the only one with no interest in paper work.

I watched the piglets play, searching for food or getting dirty, while Raphael explained to the professor the essence of what had happened. He was not interrupted. The professor was an excellent listener. He only spoke once Raphael had finished.

"Do you have any information on the cryptids they had?"

Raphael took the evidence bag with the fecal matter from his pocket. "This is what we got from one of the transport boxes we secured. I had hoped you could help us analyze it."

"Sure, sure." Professor Whiteberg nodded. "It may take a while, though. Do you have any further information to help us narrow the search down?"

I looked at Raphael. How much was I supposed to tell the professor? What was to be kept secret? He nodded for me to go ahead. "I saw three of the creatures", I said. My voice was even and matter-of-fact.

This information seemed to surprise the professor. I turned to him and watched him frown. He studied my face. "Can you describe them?"

"The first one, I was told, was a tsugo – tsuchimo …" I hesitated. What was the name again?"

"A tsuchigumo?", the professor asked. "A kind of giant spider?"

I nodded. The memory made my heart race. "The tsuchigumo was locked up again after the first fight. I do not know what happened to it."

"Can you describe it for me?" Professor Whiteberg was fascinated. "Tsuchigumo are almost impossible to keep in captivity. I hope these people know what they are doing. The poor creature, in a situation like that, so much stress …"

"It killed a woman", I said.

The professor thought about that for a moment, nodded. "You have a right to be upset, I guess. Still, do you remember any details?"

I gave a brief description of everything I remembered. It was not much.

The professor scribbled something on a wrinkled piece of paper. Once it became evident that I did not know anything else of value, he started asking about the second cryptid.

"I did not learn the name. It looked like a bog ugly mutt – or a sloth, maybe. Brown. No eyes."

"No eyes? That is interesting. Which senses did it use?"

"Not sure, either hearing or sense of smell. Maybe both. It was about this tall." I held my hand up to my waist.

The professor shook his head. "This description is not helpful. Maybe it was not even a cryptid, but a normal mammal."

Well, I would not call this a "normal" mammal. "Be that as it may, it is dead. And the third one was a scorpion."

"A scorpion? How big?"

"The size of a Shetland pony, from ground to back. The tail was longer, of course."

"What color did it have?"

"Pale, a cross between yellow and amber." I tried to think of something. "The venom was opaque and burned the skin."

"That was to be expected. The countries south of the Mediterranean Sea have various kinds of giant scorpions. Most live in the mountains, with little oxygen and extreme temperatures." Professor Whiteberg continued writing on his paper. "If we find scorpion excrements in your samples, I will be able to tell you more about the species. The rules are pretty strict for transport of most giant scorpions."

"Would it be possible to smuggle such a creature into the country?", Raphael asked. He had been silent for so long I had almost forgotten that he was here.

The professor thought about his question and finally shook his head. "I don't think so. Wild ones are almost impossible to catch, and every single one born in captivity comes with a certificate. The numbers on the documents help track the animals, and if one dies it has to be documented in a central file."

"So no one steals the certificate?", I guessed.

"Exactly."

Someone knocked on the door.

Professor Whiteberg leaned back in his chair. "Come in, please."

The door opened and a young man entered the room. His head was a nest of golden curls. "The analyses are done, Professor."

I turned towards the window and watched the reflections of the people behind me. My heart was pounding inside my rib cage like a prisoner trying to escape.

"Very well." The professor smiled. "I'll be there in a minute."

Damn. I had seen Goldilocks before. At the arena. He had helped collect the bets. Had he recognized me?

Once the door was closed again we said our good-byes and promised to stay in touch. The professor offered to take me on a tour of the premises. I said something pleasant, shook his hand and followed Raphael back to our vehicles.

As soon as we were alone outside, I tugged at his sleeve. "He was one of them!"

"Who, the professor?"

"No!" Well, who knew? And we had just told him everything we knew. "The guy who knocked on the door. He was at the fight."

"That's not good." Raphael frowned. He must have arrived at the same conclusion as I had.

"Will you have him arrested?"

He shook his head. "If they don't know that we do know, we have an advantage over them. Maybe they'll let something slip."

"That only happens in movies", I said.

"How do you know?", he shot back. "Are you the crime expert?"

If he wanted to have it his way ... I grabbed my helmet and put it on my head. "Okay, we'll see." The engine roared, and gravel shot through the air as I drove off. First I would go home. And then ... we would see.

Chapter 8: Bending the law

Instead of turning right at the end of the street on the hill, I chose the other direction. The fridge was empty, I had to stop by the grocery store. Since December, Falk had been taking care of these trivial affairs – and I had gotten used to these luxuries in no time, it seems. Fortunately, the store was rather empty in the afternoon, only a few old people and a group of sweating teenagers coming from soccer practice were blocking the aisles. I did not mess around, but want for the frozen food section straight away. Eating various kinds of frozen pizza was wholesome nutrition, I was sure. But when I stood in front of the freezer, I had a hard time making up my mind. Nothing looked appetizing. In the end I grabbed a random box and headed for checkout.

While I was waiting, I browsed the headlines of the press. "News", they called it. A pregnant Swedish princess. The local soccer club losing again. Beer would sell like crazy. I completely ignored the most famous newspaper, but the local variety had pictures on the front page that drew my eye. KUIPERS MANAGEMENT FAIL AVERTED, the headlines read. Below there was a picture of the regionally famous ship owner, Theodor Kuipers, getting out of the limousine in a fancy suit. His grey hair let his scalp shine through under the power of the photographer's flashes. Still he looked satisfied. And most of all he looked familiar. I hesitated, and some grandma almost ran me over with her cart. I wondered where I had seen that guy recently. I pulled a newspaper out of the shelf and put it down in front of the cashier with the pizza to pay for both. Then I hurried back home as fast as I could. I was starving.

Under normal circumstances I would not take the bike for such a short distance. At the traffic light I accelerated and had to brake almost right away, as I was home already. I drove up the curb, pushed the BMW past the garden gnomes and parked it close to the wall. The gnomes would take care of it. The "Magic behind the mountains" plaque was tilted again. Looked as if we had moles. A few tulips held up their leaves like blades. I put the key in the lock and let myself inside.

Marias jacket was still hanging in the hallway. Falk had recently added a second, lower row of hooks at a level she could reach more easily. For a moment I stared at the screws like a numb moon calf. Not even Strega could cheer me up, although she was doing her best by rubbing against my legs with grim determination. Red and black cat hair started accumulating around my ankles.

"Maria, I need to use the computer!", I called while I took off my jacket.

"No problem, just a moment!", she shouted back.

Walking past the stairs I saw my assistant with a giant heap of papers piled on the desk. Her smooth black hair caressed her shoulders. She did not look up when I entered the room. Instead she marked dates in my calendar with a pink marker. "These are the next appointments for the conference center. The investors have decided a smudging ceremony will take care of the project."

"Isn't it wrong to take their money?" I knew as well as the next guy that the project was not crashing due to Korean ghosts or a curse. Stupidity and incompetence were more than enough to turn a million dollar investment into a liability.

"You could do some *pro bono* work."

I laughed. "The city is not that poor." I could donate the money to a good cause. Tomorrow, however, I would talk to the mayor. And not only about Korean investors. "Why are you still here, by the way?"

"Just wanted to make sure you've got everything you need before I leave."

"That's nice of you, I'm fine." I waved with the frozen pizza to prove my point.

Maria shook her head and drove towards the main door. "Call me if you need anything, okay?"

She was the best. I smiled and turned on the computer. "I will, promise."

When the door closed I went into the kitchen, switched on the oven and tore open the pizza box. The dough was already starting to thaw. A quick search did not turn up any parchment paper, so I put the pizza on the naked baking sheet. Then I fed Strega, glanced at the watch and returned to my desk.

A brief internet research did not turn up much. Kuipers was an old family business and had hit a rough spot, like all other shipping businesses, some time ago. Theodor Kuipers was the last male heir and seventy-three years old already. Maybe he planned to keep everything under control until the end. I read the short texts on their homepage and the family history on Wikipedia. The only thing worth noting was the number of routes they offered. Of course they worked from Rotterdam in the Netherlands as well, which was just a few hundred miles down the river, but they also offered help with customs in Amsterdam. From the Netherlands they crossed Germany and ended in Switzerland. They also offered truck services, but did not put much effort into that part of their business. All in all they were like any other shipping company, except for the fact that they held on longer than most. Over the last four years, I read, more than a dozen had closed shop.

The smell made me return to the kitchen – barely in time. The crust was pretty dark already, but the cheese was golden and bubbly and not black. I pulled the pizza onto a plate and looked at it in confusion. Pepperoni? I did not even like pepperoni pizza. Where did I have my thoughts? Ah well, hunger is the best cook. And if everything failed, I could still grab some shawarma from town. I picked up the plate, gave it an evil stare and carried it to the living room. Surely there would be some dumb TV program to distract me.

After fifteen minutes I gave up and switched off the TV. I had eaten the pizza, somehow, without realizing it. I was not in the mood to stay glued to the sofa. My fingers were itching. I needed to do something. I pushed the empty plate aside, stood up, walked into the office and back. Then I grabbed my mobile and called Raphael.

"What's up?" He sounded distorted. Had he been sleeping already? It was only nine.

"Are you busy?", I asked, feeling guilty.

"Helena?"

"I know someone else who was at the fight."

At least that got his attention. "Spill it."

"Theodor Kuipers."

"The ship owner?" Raphael did not sound as if he believed me.

"Exactly. I saw his picture in the papers."

Raphael was silent for a moment. Then he said, "How old is he? Must be close to eighty."

"Seventy-three", I corrected him.

"And at that age he goes hiking with monsters? Are you sure?" He coughed. "Listen, Helena, yesterday was pretty tough for you. And I bet you haven't been sleeping properly since."

I did not believe my ears. "Do you think I'm wrong?"

"I think … I think you should rest. Take a nap." He hesitated. "Do you have someone you could call to keep you company?"

"I don't need a babysitter." My heart was dancing with anger.

"I just think that you should not be alone right now. Not after what you've been through."

"Is that an offer?" I was almost shouting.

"Calm down, Helena. I could come over, if you want to. No strings attached. You should not be alone right now, really."

"No thanks."

He sounded annoyed. "Why are you so upset? After all you're the one you called."

"To tell you about Kuipers. Not to get some male attention." I forced myself to sound calm and reasonable. My voice was cold enough to produce ice cubes.

"I understand you, really", Raphael claimed. "You are alone and worried about your … assistant. The last twenty-four hours must have been horrible!"

And now he wanted to save me? Sorry, but he was at least twenty years too late to play knight in shining armor for me. "You're right, we should talk tomorrow." I pushed the red button and stared at my mobile phone as if I could kill him with my death stare, even ever the phone.

Then I dialed the next number.

"You missed me?" The voice was hard to understand over the static.

"Stop it, Lizard face." The anger from the last call was still waiting beneath my skin. "I need information on your transport arrangements."

"Not on the phone. Do you have beer?"

The question confused me. "I guess."

"Fine, I'm close."

The call ended.

Wait – how did he know where I lived? After a moment I remembered that his buddies had kidnapped me from the woods around the corner last fall. Next question: Did I want someone like that to come and visit me?

Strega appeared in the doorframe, jumped on the sofa and looked at me as if she wanted to ask: What have you done to my favorite human? Ever since Falk had moved in with us, she had been sleeping next to him on the sofa. Or curled up at the foot of my bed when we … well. I felt my cheeks turn red. I extended a hand to scratch that spot behind her ear. She closed her eyes. It almost looked as if she was smiling. After a few moments she had enough, pulled away from me and hissed. Then she started cleaning herself.

I got up to take the plate back to the kitchen when the doorbell rang. My goodness, he must indeed have been close. What was he doing around here at this time of night? This was not your usual ghetto. I opened the door, plate still in hand.

Lizard Face was wearing his usual black hoodie and oil-stained denim pants. He grinned, but made no effort to enter.

We stared at each other for a moment before I understood.

The protection spell. Of course.

"Come inside, feel at home", I mumbled, turned around and went into the kitchen. His steps followed me.

I had fixed a spell of protection to the doorstep when I first moved into this house. It kept people who were not explicitly friendly from entering. Unless I invited them in. Kind of like vampires. When Maria had broken into the place to apply for the position as my personal assistant, I had at least known that she was not planning anything darker than that. Yeah, that was the way I arrived at most of my decision. And so far it had worked, right? Still I had added an extra layer of protection against break-ins after that.

138

The chaos on the working surface had not yet gotten out of hand. No surprise there, after all I had hardly been home all day. I dropped the plate in the sink. The empty pizza box landed next to the paper recycling bin. I opened the door of the pantry, bent down and opened a six-pack.

"Take this." I pushed a dark brown bottle into Lizard Face's hand.

"What's that?"

"Beer." I took another bottle for myself. Maybe it would help me sleep.

"That's no beer."

"It's black beer." I walked past him, opened a drawer and started looking for the bottle opener.

"Don't you have Frueh Koelsch?"

"I didn't know people actually drink that stuff. Do you want me to brew you some chamomile tea instead?"

Of course he could not let that stand. With grim determination he held the bottle out to me. I opened it. A faint hiss escaped the bottle. Next I opened my own and took a sip – dark, bitter and with a hint of caramel. My favorite. I had never developed a taste for the local brews. Riverton had its own "River Brew" which could only be bought in special shops in the city, and Cologne had several dozen breweries, if the rumors were true. I had a taste for stronger beers. Maybe it took a few generations for people to settle for the light local fare. Maybe if I had children who grew up here, one day …

Don't go there, I told myself.

Lizard Face followed me into the living room and dropped on the sofa. I waited for his feet to come up on the coffee table, but he behaved. Still Strega kept her distance. She looked at him from all sides and raced off when he bent forward to pet her. Two jumps brought her to the top of the book shelf, where she hunched down and hissed at him.

"Quite a bitch, your kitty."

"Yeah, two peas in a pod", I answered and sat down so I could watch him. "How do you bring your drugs to Riverton?"

"Not so fast, sweetheart. What's in it for me?"

I caught a row of scales pushing through the skin of his neck, growing towards his cheekbones. In the dim light they looked grey. His eyes changed, amber bleeding out from his pupils. No white was left. In the end his pupils grew to slits. Nothing human was left in those eyes.

"You know this doesn't impress me." I almost choked on the words. Still my voice was even. Only my fingers turned to ice.

"That's good. I want you to work for me."

"Forget it. I won't do anything illegal." I put my beer down on the table.

"Who's talking about doing illegal work?" He smiled, leaned back and draped his arms over the back of the sofa. His fingernails turned to claws.

I forced my gaze to rest on his face. Don't panic. Severe emotions tended to mess with my magic. I found a spark of energy in the pit of my stomach and started nursing it, at first to the size of a marble. "What kind of work would you have for me that is not illegal?"

"Oh, just small stuff. You could help keep our secrets secret. Or help our business along with a money spell."

"Proper witches stay away from money spells."

"Are you a proper witch?" His smile widened to a grin. "And if, let's say, I needed someone to help me find out if someone else was speaking the truth …" He bent forward. His movement reminded me of angry iguanas I had seen at the zoo. "From what I see, you have no other choice."

"What makes you think so?"

"Without our help, you'll never get your guy back."

"It's all just a matter of time."

"But time is something you do not have." He named a sum. "Consider this a monthly fee. And you won't have to do anything that goes against your witch's honor."

So much money made my ears ring. If I took the offer, I would never again have to raise some grandpa from his grave so he could tell us where he hid the silver spoons. I swallowed. "Will you put it in a contract?"

"Why do we need a contract? We're people of honor." He held out his hand.

Like a bunny hypnotized by the snake I stared at his claws. He only had to grip my wrist tightly to separate my hand from my arm. I did not doubt this for one second. And I liked my hand.

Still we shook hands.

Lizard Face's skin was dry and like leather. He flexed his fingers briefly. The bones in my hand crunched, but my face stayed still like water. I pulled a piece of energy off the spark I had nursed under my breast bone and sent it flying.

His eyes flickered, and all of a sudden I could see white around his irises once again. He smiled. "For a chick, you're pretty tough. What do you want to know?"

"Well", I leaned back and sipped my beer to calm my nerves. "How do you bring your drugs to Riverton?"

"We have plenty of options."

"Do you use the river as well?"

He nodded.

"What are the border controls like? Are they strict?"

"Less strict than those for airplanes. More like truck controls."

So that was what the EU had done for us. "Do you have your own boats?"

"Of course not, that would be too bad a cover. Some business men owe us favors. Tit for tat."

"Theodor Kuipers?"

Lizard Face frowned. "What about him?"

"Does he work for you?"

"No, the old guy is pretty straightforward. Years ago some … gang member tried to sell him insurance, so to speak. Kuipers sent his own security guards after him.

That's how Thomas got into business, when his boss ended up in hospital."

"You're pretty sure there's no dirt under his fingernails?"

"Of course there's dirt. Same for everyone. He just doesn't work for us."

Unlike me. "Who does he work with?"

"I'm pretty sure he's making his own mess." Lizard Face emptied his beer. "There's no other explanation for why his business hasn't sunk yet. But I do not have proof."

Damn. I would not be defeated this easily. "Do you know what they transport on these ships?"

"Whatever needs transporting, I'd guess. Sometimes they do university work, they say. He specializes in expensive equipment and dangerous substances."

I made a mental note that I would have to do some research. Maybe Professor Whiteberg was among his customers as well. "Are there other shipping businesses you do not work with?"

Lizard Face laughed.

"I will need your help then. I have to know whether any of them ship large animals from out of country." After all, Kuipers was not the only one left. And him being there did not necessarily mean he was involved with the fighting business. I had seen the mayor there as well.

I got up, grabbed the beer bottles and brought Lizard Face to the door. As soon as he was outside, I said, "Thank you very much for your visit." It might sound too formal, but I breathed a sigh of relief. This was the proper way to revoke my invitation and activate the spell of protection again. Until next time.

Lizard Face put a hand in his pocket and handed me a business card. "Here, you're family now. This is my private number. Memorize it and burn the card. I'll talk to some people and call you tomorrow. Just don't say a word to your police buddies."

"I'm not that stupid!", I called after him.

He did not react, just got in his car and drove off. The engine was hardly audible in the evening quiet. His tail lights disappeared between the trees and down the hill.

Well, maybe I was stupid after all. I had a deal with a local gang. They were probably not worse than my usual clients. I thought of the mayor with his open smile and the betting slip in his fingers when the unknown fighter lady died. My anger raised its head. I would take care of that tomorrow. And when I got home, my new business partner might already have left a clue how to get Falk back. Just follow the big animals.

Chapter 9: Never say never

If this was what ageing felt like, I could do without. Only one beer, and already the next morning my head felt as if I had slept in a screw clamp. I pulled the blanket over my head to block out the spring sunshine. Life was not fair.

On the nightstand, my phone buzzed and beeped and danced without mercy. I continued playing dead. The alarm could go fuck off. After I got up. Which would be around noon.

A determined THUMP, and my phone continued its slightly distorted dance on the floor. Reluctantly I pushed a corner of the blanket aside and found myself eye to eye with Strega. She looked very content. Seemed she had redecorated. Maybe that was a sign. Of course it was a sign. It said: Feed me. Witch cats were really good at this sort of magic trick.

Eyes half closed, I chased the phone across the floor and pushed buttons until the buzzing stopped. Then I looked at the display, realized what time it was and considered going back to sleep. Half past six, really? Well, not much to be done about it. If I had set an alarm for this early, I had probably had a plan. And once I had coffee, I might even remember it.

Strega followed me downstairs, tail held up high, and kept getting in my way until I had filled her bowl. Of course she did not eat her food – only looked at it with disgust, then ran into the hallway and curled up on the table next to the door. No idea why she had been so annoying only moments before. At least she seemed happy now.

Brewing coffee was something I could do in my sleep, which was good. Only the smell of the dark liquid gold brought me to my senses. The last thirty-six hours had been one hell of a ride. I stared out the window without actually seeing anything. The old man living at the end of the street was already out for his daily stroll. He looked my way and shook his head. I waved half-heartedly. Then I remembered that I was only wearing underpants and ran back upstairs to get dressed. I did not want Maria to suffer a heart attack. I would never find such a good secretary again.

My wardrobe still held a decent pair of faded grey denim pants. At first they were a bit snug, but after a few adventurous moves they shaped to match my curves. I chose a green and orange tie-dyed shirt to go with it which I had gotten from my mother's drum circle as a Yule present a few years ago. These hippie clothes were always a bit more comfortable, so no one had to worry about the appropriate clothing size in gifts. And indeed the top was wide enough to make me look fragile. It hade luxurious batwing sleeves and, when I stretched, revealed my bellybutton. From a drawer I grabbed an old white leather belt with a golden belt buckle. In this outfit I felt prepared for everything – even statesmen visits, if need be.

Statesmen … now I remembered why I had planned to get up this early. I wanted to go and see the mayor. If I was at the city hall early enough, I did not even need an appointment. I had a key card, and I knew he preferred to have a quiet second breakfast at his desk. With the things we had to discuss, I expected him to choke on his croissant.

The coffee did not help much to wake me up. On a perfect day I would curl up on the sofa with a good book. Instead I put my hair in a ponytail, grabbed my protector jacket and helmet and was on my way by seven. I wanted to be ahead of rush hour traffic.

The sky over my head was as blue as a robin's egg. The motorbike purred to life and rolled out into the street as if by magic, curving down the hill under lush green trees.

The city hall was teeming with life. Good thing I did not have to make it past the official visiting hour crowd. Instead I left my BMW in the personnel parking lot and used a tiny elevator with mirrored walls. I was met by the familiar, disgusting coconut smell – an artificial perfume that got stuck in my pores. With help of my key card I set the elevator in motion and held my breath until I reached the desired floor.

The people in the offices I passed did not pay me much attention. They had gotten used to my occasional appearance. Most of the time I disappeared after a few minutes, having talked to the mayor, and did not interrupt their day-to-day life. I stepped out of the way of a woman with a huge tower of files in her arms which left only her black curls visible. She had not noticed me, it seemed. Then I opened the door to the anteroom of Sterling's office.

His personal assistant frowned when she saw me, but she knew the procedure too well to try and get rid of me. She had a personal aversion against people working magic. We ignored each other with polite smiles every time we were in the same room. Now she grabbed the phone, pushed a button and said, "Miss Willow is here – does she have an appointment? Okay. Yes, okay." Then she turned around and said, "You can go inside. I will get the coffee."

This sentence had to hurt her to the core.

Mayor Sterling sat behind an empty desk and smiled. He always seemed happy to see me. Usually I liked him well enough – but not today. I knew now what kind of events he visited in his spare time.

"Helena, what brings you here?" He got up and walked around the desk to shake my hand. I kept my distance. That was the hand that had held the betting slip.

"I know where you were two nights ago."

His face did not betray anything.

"Near the monastery. I've seen you – I was there as well."

His gaze started to flicker.

"You lost money when the woman died."

Talking about the dead fighter made him flinch. His eyes darted past me, to the door.

I expected him to hold his finger up to his lips. He would not silence me this easily. "I always considered you to be a decent person."

"That was just sports", he tried to explain.

"That was not sports, but murder." I felt anger in my stomach, called by my anger. "And all those rich people standing around dreaming of fat purses. What were you doing there, shaking voters' hands? Or was the money from the bets meant to cushion your election campaign?

"Helena, listen – as mayor sometimes I have to do things I would rather not do."

"Oh no, don't act as if you have suffered. I am a witch, remember? I know when you're lying."

"Using magic against a person without consent is illegal."

148

"Then why don't you go and call the police? I bet they would be very interested in our story."

He acknowledged defeat. "Fine, what do you want?"

I wanted to break his nose, but after years of cooperation it would probably have been out of place. "I want you to not run for re-election."

"Since when have you been interested in politics?"

"I want you to publicly acknowledge that you will leave office at the end of this term." I also wanted to throw him out of the window, but I kept my calm. Even if he stepped down right away, re-elections would only take place a few weeks earlier than the usual elections – and this change of appointments would cost the city a fortune.

I was not sure whether the next mayor would be as welcoming of witches and magicians as this one had been. The city had been one of my best clients. Sterling had initiated many positive changes for the likes of us. But none of this was enough to make up for his expression when he watched that woman die in the ring. And even if the next candidate was just as much of a scoundrel as Sterling – after all it was a prerequisite for running for office – I wanted this one gone.

"You have one week to make the announcement. After that I will send an anonymous note to the press."

"Helena, you don't have any proof."

"How do you know? Modern cameras are tiny enough to fit in a purse – or a wig." Of course I was bluffing. But if I could make him believe that I had undermined this secret society on my own, he surely believed that I had collected material as well. He was not one to risk anything.

We stood right in front of each other. None of us had moved while we spoke. When the oor opened we rushed apart like secret lovers meeting at the water cooler. I smelled fresh coffee – the good stuff, a real delicacy – and felt regret for a moment. I would probably not drink it again. I would also miss the fancy cups they used here. This would mark the end of a major chapter in my life, and I was not yet sure what would come after this.

Sterling cleared his voice. "Fine, I suggest you present your assessment on the conference center project by the end of next week. It is probably in the interest of all parties involved to close this file in a timely manner.

I nodded and forced myself to smile. "I concur. We have achieved everything possible by magic."

The secretary looked at us. Maybe she felt that something was going on. But she was way too professional to ask questions while I was in earshot.

"Too friendly of you", I refused the coffee she offered, "but I have to meet someone." No matter how good the coffee, I did not intend to stay in a room with this monster any longer than was absolutely necessary.

There were other monsters I could do business with. And after everything I had learned about the mayor, Lizard Face and his buddies were more to my liking.

It was easier to leave the parking lot than to get home. I was stuck in rush hour, and the main street was jammed. Instead of going fifty and rushing from one quarter to the next, I did some traffic light hopping. At snail pace. Maybe

I would be faster if I pushed the bike on the sidewalk. I looked at the fuel gauge – my baby had developed quite a thirst over the last few days. Luckily I was only a few steps away from the gas station. As soon as the column started moving, I pulled into the station, cut off a few cyclists and braked in front of the gas pump. If they had something to say about my riding style, at least I could not hear it under my helmet.

I switched off the engine and pulled off my helmet. Sweat plastered my hair to my forehead. Filling the BMW up did not take long. The numbers on the gas pump made me sweat even more. Quite an expensive hobby. And when I started digging for my wallet in my backpack, I felt a familiar vibration under my fingers. My phone was ringing.

It was a local number. I held the phone to my ear. "Hello?"

"Miss Willow?"

I knew that voice. "Professor Whiteberg! Do you have any news for me?"

"That's why I'm calling. Could you come by the institute?"

I hesitated, open backpack in my hand, still holding the nozzle. If the professor was involved in this affair, I would be stupid to go there on my own. However, Raphael had been very clear on this: He wanted me not involved in the investigation. And Falk had been gone for so long … time to get moving. "Right now? Sure."

The boy behind the cash register smiled as I handed him my credit card. "Cool bike."

What did you say to that? Small talk was not my strong suit. "Thank you." I smiled back at him, put my wallet back where it belonged and drove off to the Institute of Cryptozoology. I took the back streets, saving a considerable amount of time. Tiny houses, rails, the wood-covered mountains in the distance. As long as I kept them to my right, I was going in the right direction. Maybe I was not even faster than if I had used the main street, but at least I got to move. I passed a roundabout and braked just in time to miss a van shooting out of a driveway.

Two traffic lights and several crossings further, I had reached the hillside with the institute. Coming from this side, I first passed one of Riverton's many prestigious private schools. High green wire fences, covered in ivy, separated school and university institute. This might be one of the reasons why the institute was kept secret. Who knows what all the rich parents would say to their children being educated next to a place where they bred monsters?

The gate opened as I pulled into the driveway, and the professor was waiting for me at the top of the stairs as I neared the house. "You're just in time for the show!"

I left my helmet with the bike and followed him around the estate. We were surrounded by lush greenery. After a few moments the gate had disappeared. I started feeling uneasy. Then I heard voices and was flooded with relief. At least we were not alone. Well, this did not have to be a good thing. What did I know about the professor, after all?

We entered a kind of patio between several small buildings with dust-covered windows. It was closed off by a fine steel net over our heads. Two young men pushed a box through a wired gate on a cart. We followed them. Professor Whiteberg closed the door behind us with great care. I looked into the box and saw several piglets squeaking inside. They might be the very piglets I had seen through the professor's office window last night?

A young woman was waiting next to one of the doors. The professor signaled with his right hand, and she threw the door wide open. A dark shadow raced at us and flung itself at the sky.

I ducked. My shields sprang to life.

The professor next to me smiled. "Most people are scared when they see Rockabella for the first time."

"Rockabella?" I did not understand.

He pointed at the shadow in the sky. "A Syrian rock gryphon. We are testing the intelligence of the species."

A rock gryphon, amazing – like the legendary bird from the Sindbad stories. I squinted and tilted my head back. "I thought they were larger."

"Rockabella is only five months old. She is from a procreation program at the Moscow zoo."

And she was beautiful.

The young woman whistled a melody, and the bird returned to the ground. Depending on the way the light touched her feathers, they were either grey or violet. Her beak, as I could see up close, contained sharp teeth, and razor-like claws shimmered at the end of her wings. I had never seen a bird like her before.

One of the men grabbed a piglet from the box and threw it into the ear. The squeal rose a notch.

Rockabella screamed, raised her head on her snake-like neck and plucked the piglet from the air. It squealed one last time, then all we heard was the crunching of bones. Blood dripped on the floor. I felt faintly sick.

Once the rock gryphon had finished her snack, the spectacle was repeated twice. The young woman let her rise into the air and called her back with a whistle after a moment.

"We are at the beginning of the series with her", the professor explained.

"I'm impressed. I did not know rock gryphons could be trained at all."

"Only if they are raised by hand. The Russians separate the chicks from their mother from the beginning. That makes these birds perfect for science. Rock gryphons who are not used to humans are too wild to work with them."

I felt sorry for the birds. And for the piglets Rockabella was tearing into pieces with wild enthusiasm. I looked down at the floor, where the red spot grew.

"Enough for today", the young woman decided after a while. She put a leather hood over the bird's head and carried her back into her cage.

"Why the mask?", I asked.

"Rock gryphons are born escape artists. We have to keep her from seeing the locking mechanism."

That was a bit over the top, maybe. Or he expected the intelligence of these birds to be higher than I did. On the other hand, he was the expert, and I was only a witch with a bunch of questions. "Was that why you called me?"

"Of course not. Let's go to my office. I have found something."

I hoped he really did have answers for me – or at least hamsters juggling while riding a unicycle. That would make up for the waiting and the piglets.

His office had not changed much. I sat down in the visitor chair and waited for the explanation.

"Last night I went through our transport lists for the last months", the professor started after a while. "And I found some weird entries." He took a piece of papers with tiny scribblings and shoved it towards me. "Look at the entries I marked."

I did not even try to make sense of all the weird abbreviations, but there was one word that jumped at me. TSUCHIGUMO. I pointed at it. "I didn't know you have one of those."

"We don't." The professor frowned. His scalped glinted through his receding hair under the harsh neon lights. "I have checked the lists several times – there are dozens of entries I cannot explain. There are no bills or any other papers on the animals, but they have definitely gone through customs."

"How were they transported?", I asked, although I thought I knew the answer.

"Most came by ship, via Amsterdam, and were transported by Kuiper."

I knew it. The old man had not just been there as a spectator.

"My assistant Markus signed off on all these transports."

Markus? Did not ring a bell for me.

"You met him briefly, yesterday", the professor reminded me. "He brought some papers when you and –"

"Goldilocks!", I shouted.

The professor looked at me as if I had gone mad. Then he nodded. "You're right, I assume. This morning we tried to call him when he did not show up. He should have been in charge of shipping off some samples."

Damn, he must have known we were getting close. "Did you sent anyone to his place?"

The professor seemed really happy with himself. "We sent your police friend over this morning. They haven't called us back yet."

And of course Raphael hadn't told me anything, either. This was the reason why I preferred to play on my own. And while we were at it ... "Why, do you think, are they shipping all these animals through Amsterdam?"

"Easy enough to explain, their customs have the most experience handling cryptids and all necessary means to take care of ... let's say, more exotic samples, during quarantine."

Amsterdam was only about two hours by car from Riverton. Maybe I should take a closer look at the town.

There was only one problem – witches were strictly forbidden from entering the Netherlands without written permission issued by the authorities. And it took forever to get all the right signatures and stamps. Neither Falk nor I could wait this ling.

I said my good-byes as quickly as was possible under these circumstances. With Goldilocks gone, I had to be quick. I drove home and chased the thoughts in my head. I would have to cancel all appointments and find a way to sneak into the Netherlands. They were pretty strict about all things magic – quite surprising, after all they did not worry too much about other kinds of entertainment. I knew that the death penalty was the automatic sentence for all crimes where magic was used. Foreigners, if they were lucky, were just shipped back to their country. And every professional magic worker, like me, had to register before entering, give their reason for travelling, provide their planned route and contact persons for emergencies. One of many reasons why I had never visited the tiny country. Their cheese could not be good enough to make up for all this nonsense. But now it looked as if I was running out of options.

Maybe there were online resources I could use, I switched off the engine and stayed seated on my bike, unable to move. It might be too late for Falk already. But I could not afford to think like this – not if I wanted to find the guys behind this madness. And maybe I would get my own miracle …

I had not expected to be alone at home. Today I was even glad to have Maria close. She sat in the office when I entered the living room and was sorting through tax-relevant information-

"I may have to leave for a few days", I said.

"Found any trace of Falk?" Maria sounded downright excited.

"Maybe." I hesitated, unsure what to tell her. I did not want to get her involved in my illegal plans. That could mean trouble down the road. "I need to use the computer, could you take the papers to the coffee table?"

"Sure." She put the pile she had been working on in a flat box on her lap and rolled towards the door. The wheels did not make any sound on the floor.

Once I was alone, I pulled a chair to the desk and started typing. Strega brushed against my legs and jumped up onto the keyboard, but she could not distract me this time.

At first I read everything on legally entering the country. Nothing had changed since I had last checked. The cheesemongers – excuse me, the Dutch – were still as conservative as they had been in my youth. These days you could hand in your papers online, but they would take at least four weeks for processing, the site stated. I did not have that much time.

"Are you planning a trip to Amsterdam?"

My heart skipped a beat. I had not heard Maria returning.

She was sitting right next to me, reading the information on the screen. "Sorry, I just need the yellow marker." She grabbed it from the cup containing all my pens.

I closed the browser. "Don't worry, it didn't help anyway."

158

"Visa problems?" She turned her wheelchair in a tight circle. Then she dropped a bomb on me. "If you need a permit, my great uncle may be able to help."

I was beyond surprised. "How so?"

"He is head of a conservative catholic church in Amsterdam and knows Madame Santé. She may surely get you all papers quickly."

Oh yes. She could do that. Madame Santé was the top authority for all things magic, and a world-famous voodoo priestess at that. I had read several of her books as a teenager. My mother adored her. "Why does your great uncle know Madame Santé?"

"They attend council meetings together. I do not think he likes her, if that is what you were thinking."

"So why should she do him a favor?"

"Out of curiosity, of course." Maria looked at me as if I was exceptionally stupid. "After all you are a star."

A star? I would not have used that word. But if Maria said it would help me … "How long do you need to sort this out?"

"I'll call him right away. We should know tonight." Then she rolled back into the living room. I watched her leave, shaking my head. Should it really be this easy? I really owed the Christian god for sending her to my home. And now I needed a reassuring cup of coffee.

Chapter 10: Voodoo queen

The elevator of the heavily secured building took us up to the top floor. Its floor was carpeted in a rich milk chocolate brown. But for the mirrors on the walls, I might have thought I was alone in the tiny cab. My gaze flitted over the nervous face of my secretary. Her hands kept creeping up to the gold cross at her neck, always forced back into her lap by sheer willpower.

When the doors PINGed open, she grabbed the handles at the wheels and maneuvered herself down the hallway. We had never been here before – at least I hadn't, and I didn't think Maria had had any business with the Voodoo Queen, either – but the string of dried chicken feet at the door told us which apartment we were looking for.

We advanced slowly. The wheels of her chair sank into the carpet, but I knew better than to offer Maria any help with her wheelchair. She was at least as stubborn as I was. The doors to our left remained closed, and no sound could be heard except for the quiet groan of the wheelchair material. It felt as if we were the only people in the world

As we approached, the door swung open. The hallway remained quiet. A hint of booze and decay wriggled into my nostrils. I felt queasy. Now I regretted never having taken that college course on New Old World Voodoo. Might have been nice what to expect when talking to the most powerful Voodoo Woman of Europe.

Maria's great uncle had indeed gotten an entry permit for me – if I promised to visit Madame Santé first thing after our arrival. And Maria had insisted on accompanying me. "This way I get to visit my family – and go on an adventure! Do you think I enjoy sorting through your papers all day?"

I had nothing to say to that.

Stepping over the threshold felt like walking through a curtain of jello-shots. My head spun. The sound returned with a PLOP. Someone was talking Dutch on the phone, too fast for me to understand. I had never been good with languages. The smell intensified. There was something besides death and magic in the air – chicken soup? Bile crept into my throat. Please don't let her ask us to join her for dinner.

Maria's wheels left clear lines on the floor. The carpet was dark red instead of brown here, with stains I did not want to know the origin of. Worn wicker furniture covered every inch of the floor, overflowing with bright-patterned quilts and cushions. The room was at least as spacious as the ground floor of my house in Riverton, still it felt tiny and crammed. A bead curtain separated it from what I assumed to be the kitchen, where the woman was still talking. I welcomed the opportunity to adjust and look around. Especially the view from the windows was breath-taking.

Until I realized what I was looking at. Blood swooshed through my ears.

Dead faces were staring at us from the windowsill. Some looked as if they had overslept and missed leaving together with their bodies, others were just bones and globs and maggots. Their mouths hung open in silent screams. While I looked, a crow descended from the dark blue evening sky and started pecking at a rotting cheek.

"Good evening, you must be Miss Willow. Enchanté." The voice in my back was sweet and thick as molasses and made my skin crawl.

I turned around, smile nailed into place like a shield. "It is too nice of you to meet us at such short notice. This is my personal assistant Maria."

Madame Santé was at least a head smaller than I was, with cappuccino-colored skin and a tower of tiny braids piled high on her head. Her German showed not the tiniest trace of an accent. She had a yellow wrap around and through her braids to keep them in place. Her wide hips held a long purple skirt in place. At the bottom of the skirt, lines of black and yellow human shapes were dancing with spears in their hands.

We shook hands. Madame Santé's hands were dry and rough, as if she had spent her life working. I knew for a fact that her practice was indeed hard work, although nothing you would have to get up for at the crack of dawn. For some reason voodoo was mostly celebrated late in the day. Not that I would complain if I had her working hours.

"I see you are admiring my gallery." She made a sweeping gesture to include the gruesome decoration at the window, beaming like a proud mother.

I glanced at Maria. She was pale but in control. Her eyes looked over the heads at the horizon. I was sure she was not paying any attention to the dead. "Yes, it is… impressive", I murmured.

Madame Santé appeared to be waiting for something.

To fill the silence, I asked, "I wonder why they are not facing away from your flat. Does this have a special meaning?"

"Why, of course there is", Madame Santé replied politely. "It's so nice of you to take interest in my humble work.

162

These died at my hands, and their terror feeds the Loa. But surely you have not come to talk shop."

There were hundreds of questions I wanted to ask her. This side of Dutch legislation fascinated me. People found guilty of severe offenses involving the use of magic could be sentenced to death at the hands of a practitioner – most often Madame Santé. How had she gotten this job? Had she ever doubted a decision or refused to execute someone? And did the dead trouble her at night?

Well, at least to that last question I probably knew the answer already. The priestess did not look like someone in need of sleep. But all of this was not what we had come here for. I produced a photo from my coat pocket. It looked slightly worn from all my worries. "This is my other assistant, Falk. He disappeared a few days ago, and we have reason to believe he might be in Amsterdam. Do you happen to know what fate might have met him?"

"So you need my help." The dark-skinned woman sounded weirdly satisfied. "Would you care for a drink? Tea maybe, or coffee? Or some cold refreshments?"

Maria shook her head. "No, thank you."

"Coffee would be nice, thank you." I talked fast. I did not want to anger our host. Also … coffee.

She nodded and disappeared into her kitchen. The pearl curtain clinked quietly.

"Are you alright?", I asked my assistant quietly. "Would you prefer to wait in the car?"

"I'm fine", she replied.

"You should have accepted the drink."

"I'm not thirsty."

Something hissed in the kitchen. Then a wonderful scent spread through the flat, mixing with the voodoo perfume. I felt a mix of anticipation and nausea rising inside me. In an attempt to distract myself, I turned to the window and was shocked to realize that the mouths of the heads were moving. They looked like carps. We were probably lucky that they were left without vocal chords.

Madame Santé returned to the living room, carrying a bamboo tablet with two black cups. She smiled and directed us to a seating area. Maria maneuvered around the furniture and placed herself next to the tiny coffee table. She pulled a notepad from one of the bags, and a pen. Then her hands came to rest in her lap as if she was waiting for something.

I sat down and accepted the cup that was offered.

It was the best coffee I had ever had. I closed my eyes and enjoyed the moment. It only lasted a few seconds, then I was met by an image of Falk like I had last seen him – clothes torn, blood seeping from several wounds. I did not have the time to enjoy this moment.

"So you need my help", Madame Santé repeated. "I have to admit, I was curious to meet you."

What was the appropriate reaction to this? I tried a quiet smile.

"Most of all I was curious to learn why the German authorities would settle for a parvenu like you. Don't they have proper witches in your country?"

That came as a surprise. "Excuse me?"

"I had read about you long before that dusty preacher approached me, begging for a favor. Your mother made a poor attempt to start a heritage of witchcraft from nothing."

"I assume you come from a family of voodoo priests?"

"Of course", Madame Santé replied. She set her cup down on the black saucer without a sound. "I do understand that magic has a strong pull for everyone. But it is not a toy for anyone to grab from a shelf."

"There are ancient scientific controversies on the idea of inherited magic", I disagreed politely.

"What do they know of magic?" Madame Santé made a face. "They try to measure something that is much older than their rules and laws. It is like catching a rainbow with a tape recorder. Families like mine have been caring for and protecting the essence of magic for countless generations."

I wanted to keep the conversation from getting lost in shop talk. "These families have done so much for humanity. Maybe we can discuss this later, when there is more time."

"Do you think there is anything you could tell me about magic?"

"I am not interested in telling you anything about magic", I replied. My voice held a sharp edge. I tried to swallow it back down. I needed this person's help. If she was convinced that she was a better witch than I was – fine, I could live with that. As long as she helped me find Falk. So I returned to this thought. "I am asking for your help."

"Prove that you deserve it, then."

Another move I had not expected. "What would you like me to do?"

"Tell me something about this." She pressed a tiny hard objected into the palm of my hand.

I looked at Maria. I could not tell whether she was feeling any less well than before. Her pen was flying across the paper. I had no idea what she was writing down. Maybe it had not been wise to bring her after all. This meeting did not go as I had hoped.

With a deep breath I closed my eyes, turning the object between my fingers. It was some kind of figurine made from smooth wood. The head was long and narrow, with overproportionally large ears. It was cowering, with stick-like arms and legs, holding a rod in one hand. The style reminded me of the shapes I had seen dancing on Madame Santé's skirt. But when I kept searching, there was nothing else. No energy, no emotions. Maybe it had its own shields of protection? I let my energy slither over its surface and found – nothing. Had Madame Santé blocked my abilities? All my thoughts were focused on the figurine in my hands.

After a while, she asked, "What have you found?"

"This is just a cheap souvenir", I explained and opened my eyes.

Madame Santé seemed satisfied with the reply. "The tourists do not only come to Amsterdam to buy tulips and go to weed stores. My PR manager has set up a small shop where they can buy voodoo souvenirs as well. That one you are holding is Osain, Keeper of Plants."

"You could at least add a blessing."

166

"Why should I? Most people do not know what they are holding anyway."

That was quite an arrogant way to look at your customers. But that was not my problem, either. "Will you help me find my assistant?"

She nodded. "Tell me what you know."

I summarized what we had learned – every detail about the illegal fights and the cryptids being smuggled, Prof. Whiteberg's assistant and the dead found in Riverton.

"And you believe that these people have let your ... assistant live?"

"If he was dead, I'd know."

"How romantic." She smiled.

"I work with Ereschkigal. If he was with her, I would know." This woman could make fun of me all she wanted, I knew what I was talking about.

"Ereschkigal is no goddess genetically connected to you. Or do you have ancestors from between the two rivers?"

"No." I did not believe that you should only work with gods coming from the same geographic area as your ancestors. But that was just another discussion that would distract us from why I was here. Besides there was a very real risk of me angering Madame Santé enough that she would refuse to cooperate with us.

She was not too happy when I refused to elaborate. Lips pressed tightly together, she rose from the sofa and walked towards the window. Over her shoulder she said to Maria, "I suggest you wait in the hallway."

Maria looked at me, eyebrows raised.

I nodded. Whatever was about to happen here, it should not rest on her catholic soul. In addition, it increased my chance of one witness getting away if anything went afoul. We could not rule anything out after all.

Once the door of the flat had closed behind Maria's wheelchair, Madame Santé opened a window. Below in the streets I heard a streetcar passing the building. A wave of decay attacked our senses. For a moment I feared I might lose the excellent coffee I had enjoyed a few moments ago. My stomach protested. I tried to calm it by swallowing. But when the voodoo priestess lifted one of the heads from its pole with bare hands, it was over. I turned on my heel, ran into the kitchen and vomited into the sink. There was not much coming up beside coffee and bile. I kept dry-heaving. The sound echoed from the metal of the sink. I was glad that Maria had left the flat. This nightmare was mine alone – and it was not over yet.

I washed away the vomit, cleaned the disgusting taste from my mouth and took a few sips of cold water to calm my stomach. Then I could no longer delay returning to the living room.

Madame Santé looked at me, but did not say anything. She had put the decaying head on a copper plate. It was the head of a woman, maybe forty or fifty years old when she died, which had not been too long. Her eyes had started drying up and looked like dried plums. Still they started moving slowly in their sockets, as if the dead had to remember where she was. Her lips, dried out as well, pulled back over false teeth.

168

The priestess combed the straw-like, peroxide-colored hair of the dead with her fingers and bound it with a ribbon. From a small plastic pouch, she took a white powder and spread it around the head in a circle. A thick yellow maggot crawled from the dead woman's ear toward the powder. When it touched the line, it started cramping and then lay still. What kind of stuff was it?

"This one was sentenced for killing her former husband with the help of black magic. She was working in customs. Maybe she can tell us where you have to look for your … assistant."

That tiny pause in her sentences bugged me. Why did everybody think that Falk and I were in a relationship? I mean, yes, we were, more or less, but that was beside the point. I approached the table slowly while Madame Santé lit a few candles. She took a bundle of dried plants from a shelf, held it into the flames and waved it through the room. The smell of decay mixed with the aroma of the herbs and, which was weird, became less disgusting. I felt a tiny bit light-headed.

"Sit down."

Despite the awful presentation I was faced with I was also curious what would happen next. I pulled a chair closer to the table and watched a maggot crawl over one of her dry eyes. Iris and pupil were yellowish and white, and what had been white had turned a darker color than I had ever seen in a living human being. Up close I saw a tear running across her forehead, starting in her hair and reaching the neck. To both sides of the injury dried blood was still sticking to her skin. "What do I have to do?"

"Give me the picture of your young man."

169

I laid the image down in front of her and was shocked when she held it to the flames. "Wait, I still need it!"

"Take another one."

Easier said than done … but too late. I could only hope this would give me the big break-through. Without a picture I would have a hard time questioning witnesses.

Madame Santé shook a tiny rattle which made a surprising amount of noise. She hummed without a melody, and her head fell back. Her braids moved through the air like flying snakes. Then she stopped. Her hands shot forward and landed on the dead woman's cheeks. A maggot landed on the back of her hand. "Touch her", she whispered with a coarse voice.

She had to be kidding! Didn't she know how unhygienic body parts were? I ground my teeth together and extended my left hand – hesitated – moved closer to the table and the dead hand. My fingers touched the skin closely behind her ear. It felt like an old, worn wallet.

Suddenly I felt cold. The water in my stomach seemed to turn to ice. Time expanded and broke. I felt as if I was falling into darkness from great heights.

In front of my inner eye a huge building appeared, some kind of warehouse. Two trucks without label were parked next to the entrance. Dusk had settled, as if what I was seeing was taking place this very moment. I did not see anyone, but it felt as if someone was there. My instincts screamed at me to run away. Another part of me had to enter the warehouse. And then there was this disgusting smell …

170

I flinched, and a wave of heat passed over me. When I opened my eyes the voodoo priestess had sunk onto the table. The head in front of her was only mummified tissue and bone. The maggots that had been crawling over the dead woman's face only a few minutes ago looked as if they had been kissed by flames – black and brittle. They would turn to dust at the lightest touch.

I got up carefully and bent over Madame Santé. Up close she looked older than I had initially thought. I helped her from her chair, carrying most of her weight, and led her over to the sofa where she had set before. She moved carefully, with tiny steps. Up close I could see grey hair in some of her braids. They had not been there before – or had they. How old was this woman?

She stretched out with a sigh. I took one of the blankets and covered her as if it was the middle of December. "Can I bring you something?"

She nodded weakly. Eyes closed, she whispered, "Warm water with lemon, please."

I walked into the kitchen to prepare the requested drink and returned a few moments later. The voodoo priestess had not moved. The brief ritual had used more of her strength than expected, it seemed. I knew this sensation from my own work. "Does the ritual need to be completed?"

"You cannot help me", she whispered. "Now go, please."

Maria was waiting in the hall. Her wheels had left deep lines in the carpet, showing how nervous she had been. Still her face was calm and she waited for me to catch a clear thought.

Closing the door of the flat behind me took more strength than I had expected. I looked at my hands and saw them shaking. The smell of decay had settled in my clothes. My insides were hurting.

"We should take a look at custom's warehouses", I said in the end.

"What was the noise?", Maria asked.

"What noise?" I had not heard anything.

"It sounded as if you were butchering a pig. And not in a friendly, efficient way."

"Must have been part of the ritual", I replied vaguely and walked past her towards the elevator.

The doorman on the ground floor did not pay any special attention to us. I assumed that most people leaving the top floor looked as if they had seen a ghost. Or communicated with a living dead hand. He pushed a button somewhere in his cubicle behind double security glass. The door beeped and opened.

When we stood on the sidewalk, I tilted my head back and looked up. We were on the right side of the building, I was sure, but I did not see any sign of the heads. Was this because of the darkness, or was there a special kind of glamor to protect Madame Santé's ... privacy? I bet that national and international press would pay a nice sum for images of her apartment – especially those constantly speaking out against all kinds of magic and tried to depict us like lunatics drinking the blood of children every full moon.

Didn't they know that the human body was not even capable of digesting larger quantities of blood?

Chapter 11: Hippies and horror

The turn signals of the transporter we had borrowed from Maria's uncle back in Riverton blinked neon in the darkness. I opened the back door and pulled out a ramp so Maria could get inside. I was glad, secretly, that we had the car, because after half a year I still did not know much about how she solved most of her everyday problems. For example, we had attached handholds in the bathroom so she could move her body without help when she needed to use the toilet. But I had not dared ask how she took care of herself at home, in the flat she was sharing with her uncle. I was lucky, for her Dutch family had not exactly invited me to stay at their house. They did not want "evil" to enter their home. Their words, not mine. I was satisfied with this arrangement, however. Employers should keep a certain distance from their employees. And it gave Maria some time to spend with her relatives.

We drove to the tiny house in the Northwest part of the city where her family lived, not talking. The Dutch had turned living in cramped spaces into an art form. Looking through the front windows, I could see right into the tiny garden at the back. "Your family does not care about their privacy, it seems."

"Hallways and walls are considered a waste of time. And people who hang up curtains have something to hide." Maria smiled. She had the very expression I showed the world when I had to deal with my mother. You could not choose your family.

After some effort I parked the car with the back doors facing the front garden of the house Maria had indicated. In the rearview mirror I saw her great uncle and his wife stepping through the front door. Both were tall and so slim they looked almost sick. Their faces did not betray joy over our arrival. As soon as I had switched off the engine, the man opened the doors and let the ramp down. Then he climbed into the car without greeting, undid the belts and shoved Maria down onto the sidewalk.

She said something to him. Even though I did not hear a word, I recognized her scolding face. No surprise, she prided herself on being an independent woman.

I got out of the car and walked around it to close the doors again. "I'll park around the corner and pick you up tomorrow morning, then we'll drive over to customs to talk to some people." Parking in the city seemed an impossible task. I was pretty certain I would get around just nicely with the streetcar. Or I could go for a walk along the canals. After all I had never taken the time to visit Amsterdam. Supposedly the red light district was worth a visit as well. And there I might also stand a good chance of finding a bed for the night. From what I knew there were cheap hostels everywhere. All I needed was a place to put my head.

The quarter where Maria's relatives lived, and where I started my stroll, was a lovely sight. Old houses leaned towards each other across narrow streets, green was choking the walls. Many houses had been restored and decorated with colorful elements. More bicycles than cars were out in the streets – they announced themselves with ringing bells and whooshed past me without slowing down. The closer I got to the heart of the city, the shabbier the houses became, but they kept their friendly charm. The sidewalks started filling up with young people. They were washed out of alleys and bars in clouds of talk and laughter. Spring in Amsterdam, that did not only mean tulip bulbs, but also self-discovery and stag nights. I saw more bearded princesses out in these streets than would have laced a queer Disney parade. From some doors rose clouds of smoke with a distinct smell. These doors were crowded by happy people wearing T-shirts in all colors of the rainbow, having the time of their life. It looked as if I had indeed been missing out.

As I got closer to the main station, I started seeing more shapeshifters and other non-humans. Back in the living quarters I had assumed that the Dutch were rather conservative when it came to anything non-human. But around here I spotted tiny boxes and faeries flitting out of them in mists of glitter. A modern solution for an old problem – housing the wee folk in large cities. Looking into the canals I saw tiny doors between the house boats lying nose to ass. Only the top third of the doors was above the water line. I did not know who was living down there. But maybe, just maybe, I would have to change my mind about the Dutch and their fear of all things magic.

First, however, I needed a snack.

The large place in front of the station held a Febo. I had heard of those. Self-service fast food shops with addictive specialties. I pulled some coins out of a pocket and bought myself a fried cheese soufflé and some weird mashed-beef sausage. Yes, they knew how to do fast food. I tasted spices from the various countries the Dutch had colonialized in their time. Hot fat ran down my chin as I watched the people passing the shop. Even if I had not heard the language, I would have known immediately that I was not in Germany anymore. The people were blonder, the clothes more colorful – and did I only imagine it or did they indeed look happier? We might want to take a second look at legalizing marihuana.

Right now, however, the world did not hold enough drugs to make me happy. Falk would like this place, I thought. I tried to remember whether he had ever talked about having been here. No, probably not. I inhaled deeply, pushed aside all the evil emotions that had crept from my subconscious and started looking for a bed for the night.

The red light district had at least one hotel at every corner, but they were all fully booked. I should have expected this, considering the hoards of people roaming the streets. All front desks only offered a sad smile and a shake of their heads. One or two pointed me in the direction of other hotels, but everywhere I asked it was the same – the rooms were full. Street by street I walked, taking in the window displays of the shops with their smoking paraphernalia, fun condoms and young, scantily clad women vying for the people's attention. Every now and then there would be a window shop with too-sweet baked goods or fatty pieces of pizza. Each of these windows was surrounded by a hungry crowd. As it got later, I was glad I had my leather jacket with me, and solid boots. It looked as if I would have to sleep under a bridge again, after all this time.

Later I bought a paper bag of Belgian fries with "fritesaus" – what an ignorant German might have called mayonnaise. But the word did not cover the delight. The guy behind the counter shook his head, smiling at my surprise when I took the first bite, and handed me my change together with a handful of napkins. I would need those, he explained. I smiled, took everything and sat down on the edge of a canal. At my back the first tired crowds were headed back to their rooms. Others were looking for more adventures. The night was young. The cars parked along the street hid me from their view. In front of me motorboats were navigating the black waters. Drunks hollered at me. I let my feet dangle, ate my fries and thought.

The sky did not promise rain for the night. Which was good if I was to sleep out in the open. A bridge or the end of an alley would do nicely. I was getting too old for this. My bones groaned at the thought of putting my head on my backpack once more. I threw a cold fry into the water. Immediately I was surrounded by ducks fighting for a snack.

"Are you okay?", a female voice asked behind me.

I had not heard her approaching. The shock almost made me jump into the water. "Yes, yes, I'm fine. Everything's okay", I replied and turned around to look at whoever had snuck up on me.

The woman was at least fifty years old, tiny and wired. Her short grey hair was pointing in all directions. She was wearing denim pants and a rainbow-colored pullover. She held a car key in her hand. The car I was leaning against was probably hers.

When I did not elaborate, she sat down next to me and started asking questions. Her German was surprisingly good. She was called Annegriet and had been living in Amsterdam for more than forty years.

I gave her the cleaned-up version of myself that would not get her in trouble – a boyfriend who had disappeared, who had found bad company, I guessed, and my guess that he would be found in Amsterdam.

Annegriet tilted her head. "That's a bad story. Are you sure he is worth finding?"

The question made me stop. I smiled. "Definitely."

"Then I hope you will find each other."

We sat in silence for a whole.

"I have a house boat nearby – do you need a place to sleep?", she finally asked.

"It can be dangerous to follow strangers home in a foreign city", I said.

"Would you rather sleep in the market place?", Annegriet asked and raised an eyebrow. "At my place you would only have to fear me. And my parrot."

I pointed at the pentagram I was wearing around my neck. "Doesn't this bother you? Maybe I am the one you should be afraid of."

"It's a risk we both will have to live with." She got up as if everything was decided. "I was only going to get my jacket from the trunk of the car. The boat is a few hundred yards down that street, and once you're parked around here, you don't move the car unless you have to." She opened the trunk and grabbed something that looked like a tiny carpet.

I got up, slapped the dust off my pants and grabbed my backpack. "Then let's go."

It was not far indeed, and on our way Annegriet told me a few stories about Amsterdam. I forgot most of them immediately, for my thoughts still were with Falk. Which is why I almost fell into the water when we reached the footbridge leading to her boat.

"Careful", Annegriet laughed, "you'll make big waves. My boat is not meant for that kind of water." She took my arm and led me to the end of the footbridge.

From the outside the boat looked as if it had seen its share of adventures, but the inside had been repaired with a great eye for details. The boat held a single room with a cooking corner, all in white and decorated with colorful cloth and pictures that looked as if the colors had not been painted on, but had exploded. My mouth dropped open. "They are amazing. Did you paint them?"

"I paint when I have the time. And the weather has to be good, for I work outside." Annegriet put her jacket down, took a few peanuts from a tin and whistled. A large blue and yellow parrot dropped off a perch below the roof and took up residence on her extended arm. I was surprised to notice that Annegriet's pullover perfectly matched the interior of the boat. "Would you care for some tea, or a beer?"

"Beer would be nice. I am dead tired."

We sank into many-colored armchairs and continued talking about life in general and the differences between Riverton and Amsterdam for a while. I learned that Annegriet had benn in Bonn on several occasions. "Back when it was the capital, for demonstrations. I am too old to drive all the way to Berlin these days." She took a sip of her beer. "Are you into politics?"

I shook my head and stifled a yawn. "Politics is too abstract for me. I would rather surround myself with real people."

She nodded. "Many people these days consider politics some sort of game. Must be because these days you have all information at the tip of your fingers at any second. I guess it makes them nervous. They don't have time to listen to their own thoughts. But I can see that you are tired." She got up, walked to the wall and touched something I had thought to be a giant picture. It turned into a bunk, roughly the size of a slender person, with a thin mattress.

I was amazed. "Your idea?"

Annegriet nodded, satisfaction plain on her face. "I can accommodate up to eight guests. Sometimes old friends come over for a few days. We are getting too old to sleep on the floor." She grabbed a few woolen blankets from a drawer. "Take cushions from the chairs." Then she folded down a second bunk at the end of the room.

I climbed into my bed, feeling how tired I was in every limb. Through a porthole window I could see the sky lit by the city. Sometimes the boat swayed a little. I closed my eyes and was gone immediately.

The next morning we drank coffee in front of the boat, while behind us on the street bus after bus whooshed towards the main station. A seagull landed a few paces from us and tilted its head.

Annegriet threw a piece of raisin roll at the bird. "We are not supposed to feed them, the city council says. But they are my neighbors, and neighbors are supposed to help each other, right?"

The seagull snatched up the piece of roll before it hit the ground, moved its giant wings and disappeared, flying away close to the water surface.

I drank my coffee. It was strong, hot and bitter. Just the right thing to revive my senses and make a decision. Of course I would not take Maria with me today. I could not risk her life when knocking at the door of the lion's den. Besides she was the only one who could wrap up my affairs if something happened to me.

"Do you know where you are going to look for your friend?", Annegriet asked, interrupting my thoughts.

I hesitated, nodded. "Someone said he might be at the customs office."

If she was surprised by this reply, it did not show. "You may want to start at the airport."

"They say my friend arrived travelling by boat."

"Then why isn't he in Rotterdam?"

"The shipper transports exotic animals entering the EU via Amsterdam."

Annegriet made a face. "I know the procedures, from when we got Pedro."

The parrot heard its name and croaked. Annegriet threw him a peanut. She smiled. "He was a gift from a friend in the US – the only piece of him that ever traveled this far. Pedro had to remain quarantined for weeks while they tested him for all kinds of diseases and parasites. But the people were very friendly, I went there often. You might want to go to their warehouse directly, the people there will surely be able to help you if you bring a picture of your friend. We staged demonstrations there as well, years ago, protesting against the trade of ivory and corals. Not that it helped anything. It took years for the EU to ban these things, and the laws have holes you could drive a truck through. I doubt it will ever truly end." She wrote an address down on a piece of paper. "That's where you should start. But keep in mind, if your friend mingles with this sort of crowd, he might not be worth the effort."

I felt the urge to defend Falk. Annegriet did not know him, but she had been very kind. I did not want her to think I was wasting her and my time on some asshole without a conscience. "He does not work for the shipping company. It's one of his ... project. Saving animals." And avenging dead street fighters, but that was not something I wanted to burden her with.

"Do you have a car?"

Only if I went to Maria's family. "I think I'll rent one."

"Or you could take mine."

"Are you sure?" People this friendly were scary. Even if Annegriet had done nothing last night except for snoring gently.

"Here", she het the car keys dangle in front of my nose, "the gears are a bit stubborn. When you return, park it somewhere around here and get back to me."

I did not let myself hesitate, took the keys and thanked here. "It should not take more than a few hours." I emptied my coffee mug, returned it to the sink inside the boat and started walking towards the street.

"See you tonight!", Annegriet called after me, smiling. She did not look worried about whether she would ever see her car again.

I was starting to like the hippie lifestyle.

This early in the day there were not many people about on the streets and canals around the red light district. Everything was quiet. I jumped out of the way of a bike, crossed a bridge and, after a brief search, did not only find the fry shop – still closed, this early in the morning, with a heavy iron gate – but also the car from which Annegriet had gotten the jacket last night. The lock took some wiggling the key before the car door opened. I sank into dusty upholstery, closed the ashtray and opened the window. This was one ancient treasure. No surprise that Annegriet did not wonder about me stealing the car. My escape would end before we had even reached the highway, even if there was a strict speed limit all over the Netherlands. But the engine hummed a song of satisfaction, and the car crept onto the street without complaints.

With Annegriet's instructions it was no problem to find the warehouses where the bigger animals were kept after quarantine until they could continue their voyage to their final destination. From the outside, the area appeared rather boring. Several long halls with iron roofs lined a path, most with their doors slightly ajar. The street I was driving along seemed to go on forever between warehouses like this. It was pockmarked with potholes. Just another average industrial area.

I stopped at a boom gate, waiting for someone to come up to my car. I could see three guys standing nearby, all heavily armed. What were they guarding, the gold from Fort Knox? Two of them pointed their machine guns in my direction almost lazily. From now on I had to improvise. I hoped that the travel permit I had in my pocket was enough to impress the guards. I did not want much – only take a look around, talk to someone and maybe leaf through their papers. How complicated could that be?

The youngest guard came up to my car and said something in Dutch. He glared at the interior of the car. I smiled as harmlessly as possible, replied in English and held out my papers. They stated that one Miss Helena Willow was authorized to travel the Kingdom of the

184

Netherlands for work purposes. In combination with my witching permit, including stamp and German eagle, this paper was supposed to open all kinds of doors for me. After all it was signed by the Dutch prime minister, the mayor of Amsterdam and Madame Santé personally.

"This is a customs area", the officer said after reading my papers. "You need an appointment."

"I am just asking for a favor. I am investigating the smuggling of cryptids entering the EU via Amsterdam."

"And you came all the way from Riverton without calling ahead?" He frowned. "Please get out of your car."

Weird. But if he thought it was necessary … I switched off the motor, opened the door and got out. It felt good to stretch my legs.

All three pointed their weapons at me. I held up my hands without being asked.

"I had really hoped you would not come here", the young one said with a sad voice.

My brain needed a moment to sort all impressions. Wait, what were they doing here?"

"Stop!" His voice rose.

I obeyed. No way was I taking on three guys at once.

With the free hand he pulled a mobile from his pocket and dialed a number. Then he said something in Dutch, too fast for me to understand a thing. Well, I caught a few words. She's here. Contained. Hurry. Seemed they had been expecting me.

Once the call was over, he pointed his phone at one of the warehouses with the door half open. "Over there, please."

I grit my teeth, turned my back on him and walked towards the dark opening.

Chapter 12: Customs trouble

On the inside the warehouse looked surprisingly modern. Dozens of boxes were stacked on top of each other, with giant creatures moving on the inside. Floor and walls were covered in tiles. Neon lamps were dangling from the ceiling, with only every fourth switched on. Still I could see everything clearly enough – fur, scales and tentacles. I smelled predators and dust. Dense energies were swirling through the building.

I heard the steps of the men closely behind me. They were probably still pointing their guns at me. Maybe I could surprise them with a magic attack ... or they could tell me what had happened to Falk. They, or the people on the other end of the phone call I had witnessed. I would definitely get my answers.

The wall to our left looked more like a part of a laboratory than a warehouse. A work surface ran all down the wall at hip level. It was covered with test tubes, incubators and petri dishes. My guess was they had to test the mystic beasts for boring parasites as well.

We pushed past a few crates with their inhabitants hidden in the shadows. At one point I thought I smelled Sulphur. Then there was once more only fur stink. At the end of the warehouse I saw a blue light. "What is over there?", I asked.

"Tanks. Aquariums."

Aquariums? Were they breeding giant goldfish? I craned my neck to get a good look across the boxes and was rewarded with a push between the shoulder blades.

"Stop it. My boss will be angry if I have to shoot you."

Sure. And the noise would make the animals nervous. Or the smell of blood. I looked at the ground and kept walking.

In the back third of the warehouse the men made me stop in front of a crate. "Give me your necklace."

Everything inside me revolted against this order, even though I knew that my magic did not depend on a piece of metal hanging from a leather band. But the pentagram was almost a part of my body.

"Hurry up!"

I opened the clasp and dropped the necklace on the floor. For this I received another hard push.

"Hands against the box!"

He frisked me, touching my back and legs, lingering at my crotch and then travelling up over my belly and breasts to my neck and arms. He did not find anything. Of course I had been stupid enough to travel without weapons. Not that any of them would help me now. He would have ended up with all of them, and I would have had none. What a shitty situation. I was better off with no weapons at all.

"Happy?", I asked.

"Shut up!" He messed with the padlock and opened the crate I had been leaning against. "Get in!"

"I'm not crazy", I refused. Who knew what would be waiting inside?

"Get in, or I'll tell my boss you tried to attack us. Don't worry, you won't be in danger. For now."

I did not have a choice, so I obeyed. Crouched down, pushed through the tiny opening and tried to explore my surroundings with my hands as the door clanged shut behind me. Only a tiny finger of light reached the inside of the crate, everything else was black. My senses told me I was not alone. The other presence was restless and angry and …

"Helena?"

Something heavy lodged itself in my throat. My voice only worked at the second attempt. "Falk, is that you?" I felt around until my hands touched warm flesh.

"No."

"Idiot", I whispered with tears streaming down my face. Fortunately, he could not see me in here. I did not want him to think I had been worried about him.

"Are you crying?"

How did he know? "Humidity", I explained weakly. My hands kept exploring him. A leg, an arm, a hand. His skin was hot and dry. He smelled unwashed and faintly of blood. "Are you okay?"

"Could be worse. What are you doing here?"

"Looking for you."

"Well, you found me."

That made me grin. Why could they not lock me in a separate crate? This smartass! I kept moving my hands and found his shoulders, his neck. My fingers fluttered across his face in the dark, finding wet patches. I pushed against him and, lost in the moment, kissed him on the mouth. Then I said, "You have not brushed your teeth in a while."

"I've been locked up in here for days."

"You have an excuse for everything, don't you." I did not wait for a reply and kissed him again.

After a while we sat next to each other at the back of the crate, close enough that our thighs touched. "Where are we?", he asked quietly.

"Amsterdam, customs."

"I've always wanted to see Amsterdam."

I snorted. "At least you found cheap accommodations. Beds are unaffordable around here – even if you don't want anyone to keep you company. Why have they kept you alive, by the way?"

"They want me to fight for them. Do you have any idea how to get out of here?"

"We'll wait till they open the door."

"Clever girl."

I elbowed him in the ribs and felt sorry when he inhaled sharply. Medical services probably sucked in here. "The guy who pocked me in here must have recognized me somehow. He has called someone. I think they'll come here."

"And then you'll tell them to release us and hope they act reasonable?"

190

"Or trick them and escape. I guess we can decide that on the spot."

"Sounds like a plan."

Then we sat in the dark and waited. I put my head against his shoulder. Every now and again we heard something growl or hiss in the other boxes. I hoped that Annegriet would start to miss her car and call the police. Just in case we did not free ourselves in time.

The day slipped into eternity. Falk fell asleep next to me. His hair was unwashed. He smelled of sweat. We could not go anywhere right now, but that was fine with me – as long as I was with him. Whatever happened next, we would face it together.

I tried to identify the sounds whispering through the warehouse all around us. Hissing, murmuring, a sound as if someone was caressing the floor with sandpaper. Claws clicking on hard surfaces. Splintering gnawing. Heavybreathing, wet and dragging. Sometimes one of the laboratory devices buzzed to life. My imagination created monsters waiting just out of reach. I was not sure whether the images in my mind could be worse than reality. Of course we might be able to open the padlock and escape from the crate, but then what? Exotic monsters, armed officers, a foreign city, a voodoo priestess on my heels ... - not, waiting was the better alternative for the moment. And I was not the most patient person to begin with.

Suddenly there was a thump on the other side of the hall. We sat up straight, hearts pounding. Someone switched on all the lights. I was blinded for a moment. Falk's muscle tension changed and his breath caught for a second. He crept closer to the bars and tried to see what was coming at us.

"I really did not expect you to be stupid enough and stumble into this." One of the new arrivals was speaking German. I knew the voice. After a moment of hard thinking I knew who he was. Goldilocks from university. Prof. Whiteberg's assistant – what was his name again?

"You are causing us lots of trouble", he continued. "We will have to clear the warehouse – just in case you were clever enough to call for backup before you got here."

"Let us out and we'll help", I offered.

"I have my people for the job." He pointed at the men accompanying him. Two of them were giants with a facial expression reminding me of instant pudding – sticky and nothing special. The third one was wearing an expensive suit with, I kid you not, a silk handkerchief. Even from the distance I could see the price tag hovering over the fabric. I bet his brogues stayed dust-free even in here. Money had some advantages you could not get from magic. After a few hours in this box I probably looked like a rag doll left in the attic.

"Is the professor involved?", I asked to fill the silence.

"Whiteberg?" Goldilocks laughed. "He would never risk his ideals for this. That is why he is living in a room at the institute and ironing his own shirts. But he was of good use to us – after all he is why I knew you were after us. That is why my people were looking out for you."

"And now what?"

"You tell me. What am I supposed to do with you?"

"You could let us off with a stern warning."

Goldilocks shook his head, feigning disappointment. "Give me something better, Helena. I may call you Helena, yes?"

Under different circumstances I might have told him all the other things he could do to me, but I thought it more reasonable to keep my mouth shut. I was getting really good at this.

"At least you're lucky", Goldilocks continued. "My friend here, Win van Varen, wanted to get rid of you together with the live food. It is hard to get human body parts without attracting attention, and some of our investments can only eat human protein. Instead I think you are going to help us."

Sure.

Goldilocks must have read my expression through the bars. He laughed. "Don't worry, I am not going to make you do something unmoral. But I think your friend will be more motivated to cooperate as long as we have you ... to keep us company."

Damn, that might just work.

Falk raised his head and looked at Goldilocks. "Why don't you let her fight?"

Wait, what?

The other men must understand at least a little German, for their lips twitched. Goldilocks, on the other hand, appeared annoyed. "I didn't think you were such a coward."

Falk was not deterred. "What do you think happened to that giant bug in the woods? And what would people pay to see a fight between a monster and a witch? The ticket prices alone would make you a rich man, and imagine the bets!"

I gave him an angry look. Stop it! I had not tried to feed him to the wolves, either.

Goldilocks thought about it. "Maybe you're right. Seems you have a brain in that stubborn head of yours after all. Let me see her." He waved the big guys closer.

Van Varen shook his head and said something to Goldilocks in a quiet, but urgent voice.

"What are you doing?", I hissed at Falk.

"That way they'll let us out."

"And then they'll throw us to the beasts."

"Do you have any better plans?"

No, I did not, and now it did not matter anymore anyway. The men had found an agreement, and the door opened.

I crept from the box with stiff legs. When I got up, my muscles screamed their protest. How much worse did Falk feel? I did not want to imagine how long he had been stuck in here. Especially since my bladder was already pretty full.

In the meantime, our captors had made up their minds as to which investment they wanted to send against us. One of the big guys was sent away with cryptic instructions and disappeared between the crates. Something big was howling in the distance.

We stumbled down the warehouse between boxes filled with giant animals. My circulation started up again, slowly.

194

We were directed towards a tall, closed and heavily secured gate. An area of maybe fifteen by thirty feet was not filled with boxes and crates. This must be where they loaded the cryptids onto the trucks to get them to the boats. Over our heads I saw two cranes and several bright neon lights.

From one corner of the warehouse the sounds indicated restlessness. I turned towards Goldilocks. "Before we start I have to wash my face."

Van Varen spoke German, I learned, although he had a heavy accent. "Don't bother. What do you think this is, a hotel?"

I started opening my belt without taking my eyes off Goldilock's face and pulled down my zipper. His buddy was easy to ignore, he was no on our side to begin with.

"What do you think you're doing?"

"Do you really think I won't piss on your floor, right here?"

He grunted and grabbed my arm. "Don't play smart, or we'll find something else to convince your friend." He pushed me towards a narrow door with a dirty lattice window, switched on the light and gave me a shove. "Hurry, or we may start without you."

No one had bothered to clean this place in a while. I looked around. No window to the outside world. Would have been too convenient. We had ended up in quite a hassle. Well, what had I been expecting? Most likely I had only been glad to have Falk back, and to have a moment to recover. I did what I had come for. Through the door I could see the back of Goldilock's head. If only I was sure that we would handle the other three ... I washed my hands at a tiny basin, splashed some lukewarm water at my face and took a deep breath. Let's rumble.

Entering through the narrow door, I caught a quick glance from Falk and shook my head. No way out yet. My heart beat faster, and the tips of my fingers turned cold. Was this what he felt like before every fight? Thank you very much, I could do without.

Goldilocks shoved me. I stumbled into the middle of the free area. And like that we had a kind of improvised fighting pit. The only things lacking were the opponent and the spectators. Wait, had I developed a new business model? No, that honor belonged to our captors.

Between the crates I saw the head of the second big guy appear. He walked weird, but when he walked past the last crates and into the open, I knew why.

He was holding some sort of guiding cane, with an eight-legged creature on the other end. Its hairless humanoid head almost reached his hip. The monsterfought the sling around its neck every step of the way. It hissed. Sharp claws clicked on the ground. It threw itself from left to right, to no avail. The guy had trouble staying on his feet. Every now and again blue sparks flew through the air. Electroshocks. I would give my right arm for a taser.

"The asanbosam is from central Africa. It's famous for its bad mood", Goldilocks explained, as if he was talking to an audience at university. "North of the equator, breeding them is almost impossible, hence we may import a limited number. Unfortunately asanbosams are rather rare, and this far north they are not expected to survive for long. If I were you I would stay away from its fangs, their venom is pretty strong." He waved a black angular object. "If our magic flute fails, I still have the taser. We don't want our goods to be spoiled."

So that was it. Goldilocks did not expect us to survive this intermezzo. What an asshole. So then why was he doing all this to begin with? I looked at him and caught the spark in his eyes. That son of a bitch enjoyed the show!

The asanbosam tilted its head back, hissed and clicked its razor-like teeth. Its front legs swooshed through the air. Its reach was greater than expected.

Great. Besides, it was ugly and in attack mode and had as many extremities as we had combined. I guessed it was also faster than we were and could jump higher. That was not the day I had imagined.

Goldilocks blew his tiny magic flute, and the beast froze. A sad note flew through the warehouse. I had seen the effect before, and still it fascinated me. Were the monsters trained for this note or was it some kind of magic kill-switch? I watched the big guy pull the sling over the beast's head, then he retreated towards the gate. He had good survival instincts. I understood him. To be honest, I would have liked to follow him.

Meanwhile, Wim van Varen drew a wide circle around us with a white powder. He did nothing that looked like magic at all, still I felt the circle come to life as it closed. The effect had to be connected to the powder, for van Varen had no magic talent to speak of. Why had they not used it at the other locations? Seemed to be a fine solution to keep creatures inside – or outside. Unless someone disturbed the line, of course. Or if there was wind. Or rain, depending on what the substance was made of.

Be that as it may, the three of us were locked in here for now.

After one last long breath Goldilocks put the flute away.

The asanbosam shook its head and looked around.

Falk and I spread out, rounding the fighting pit in opposite directions. I did not take my eyes off my opponent. It sat in the other half of the magic circle, almost in the center, and appeared to vibrate. Its gaze wandered from left to right and back, faster and faster. It seemed to be not sure whether we were a threat or only food.

The attack came out of the blue. One moment the beast sat like a grotesque statue under the neon lights, the next it flew through the air at Falk. Maybe it had smelled the blood. Its spider legs catapulted it through the air like steel springs.

Falk saved himself with a desperate lunge and landed in his injured shoulder. He drew a sharp breath. I stood like stone – I wanted to run over and protect him, but I was afraid of the monster we were facing. The panic suffocated my energy.

Stop, there was something. I forced myself to breathe and rammed my energetic roots through the cement under my feet. The ground felt weird, like a sponge. I kept digging. And there it was. Red energy, Mother Earth, and a wave of blue energy I had only found at the ocean. Both were dancing together in a spiral of magic and flowed upward, through my feet into my legs and my center. For a split second I felt seasick. That was not what I had expected. But I grabbed everything I could get, pushed it into my center and separated the connection to the ground before I had to vomit. Once I could not control it any longer, I pushed it down my arm and ran at the beast. My fear was gone.

With the outstretched hand I touched one of its spider legs, and for the first time I experienced pure hate. It was like a black light emanating from the center of this exotic being, and it clung to everything it touched. The darkness had almost reached my center by the time I had my shields in position. My arm was cold as ice.

But my attack had been effective, for the leg I had touched crumbled under the creature's weight and spasmed. Its second jump failed, and it missed Falk by mere inches.

He in turn had not remained docile. When the monster flew through the air past him, he grabbed one of the legs and pulled it.

The beast screamed. It turned around mid-air, presented its fangs and crashed to the ground with Falk. I saw venom glistening in the dark and panicked. No!

I threw my shoulder against them to separate them. Goldilock's words reverberated through my head. Now that I had Falk back again, I could not let this … this thing chomp him to death.

The asanbosam's body seemed to be protected by a chitin shield. My fists did nothing. The monster turned its head by almost one hundred and eighty degrees and growled at me. Its breath stank of rot and decay. At this short distance, however, the fangs were even more impressive than the stink. I wanted to retreat – and stumbled over one of those terrible legs.

The hooks at the foot of the asanbosam got tangled in my clothing. I was at the center of its attention now.

Desperately I tried to free myself, missed a step and almost landed on my ass. Instead I was dragged up and closer to its terrible face. The moving fangs hypnotized me, each one as long as my lower arm. A scream got stuck in my throat. Time stood still.

A solid ball of the strange energy I had found under Amsterdam raised through my throat and cut off my air. Without connection to the ground I lost all orientation. A carousel was spinning inside my head. Soulless black eyes came closer to my face, its breath caressed my skin. I gagged, groaned, tried to breath – what was that, some kind of shock? From the corner of my eye I saw Falk scrambling to his feet. His face was a mask of pain. He moved towards us, but he was too slow. My vision seemed to melt, and everything turned dark.

When the scream unlodged from my throat, it tore all the energy I had gathered loose and threw it at the monster. Its face crumpled, dried up and blackened. It screamed, let go of me and tried to escape.

It crashed into the invisible wall of the circle and was thrown back.

Our spectators retreated, gasping. One of the big guys had a dark wet spot spreading all over his pants. I was lying on the floor and trying to catch my breath. Falk was kneeling next to me. "Are you okay?"

"Don't worry", I coughed, "go and get it!"

He hesitated for a moment. The tips of his fingers brushed against the dried up skin that had been the monster's face. Then he staggered to his feet and followed the asanbosam.

I had no idea what I had done. My magic had never felt like this. It was a good thing that we were in a circle. I did not want to imagine what I could have done out in the open … wait.

Time stretched. I saw Falk sliding across the floor and kicking the asanbosam's abdomen. He tried to get out of reach again immediately, but his injuries slowed him dowm. The monster reared over him and pushed two legs against his shoulders. One of the claw-like hooks tore into the bloody tissue. Falk screamed.

My body held more energy than I had ever thought possible. I saw the world through a blue veil. The gates to the world of the gods in my subconscious were pulled wide open. "Give me!", lion-faced Ereschkigal shouted. Her glowing eyes filled my horizon. I forced myself to let go of the energy and felt as if I was being torn apart. When the spell burned my fingers, I threw myself between Falk and the asanbosam and pushed my hand against its body. DIE, I thought – not in words, but in pictures: Torn flesh, drying limbs, wastelands and ruin. Beyond it all, Ereschkigal was smiling with satisfaction. She was cruel and beautiful.

The asanbosam coughed. It seemed to shrink as it fell in on itself above us. When its body touched mine, it was dead already. Only a crumbling hull was left. The chitin was starting to fall apart

The men on the other side of the circle line watched in horror. I hardly recognized them, as if they werc hidden by mist. The spell had not been used up completely. The air was suffocating us. I had to do something to set it free.

I rolled off of Falk, and the dead asanbosam disintegrated. Black flakes rained down on my hair. My face was close to the circle. I blew on it gently – that was all it needed. And once the line was gone, we were free.

My magic raced through the warehouse and started chaos in the crates holding all the other cryptids. They were screaming, hissing and growling, throwing themselves at the walls of their cages. And the men turned to flee.

I stretched, opened my fist and let go of a perfect spark. It flew through the air and burst into an aquarium at the end of the room. The glass broke with a sigh, and a giant, squishy body was flushed into the room. I saw fins, teeth and opaque eyes. The thing collided with Goldilocks before he could reach the door, and buried him. Then there was blood everywhere.

Wim van Varen was almost at the door when hell broke loose on the outside as well. Men with masks and machine guns poured through the gate, aiming at everything that was moving.

We froze. I could not have moved if my life depended on it. I had never felt this exhausted and wonderful at the same time. In the group of strangers I thought I spied a familiar face. I smiled and closed my eyes. I just needed to rest for a moment.

Chapter 13: Ancient curses

Returning to reality, I saw into Raphael's worried eyes. First I was disoriented. What had happened? Had I imagined everything? I tried sitting up, and every single part of my body hurt. My stomach turned, but there was nothing I could have lost. I retched and felt saliva running down my chin. Not just another ugly nightmare.

Falk, I remembered suddenly. The last time I had seen him he had been on the ground, not moving. Was he doing well? I ignored the pain and the nausea and tried to get on my feet.

Raphael pushed me back onto the floor. "Stay down, the doctors will get to you in a moment."

"What about -?"

"He's alright", he tried to calm me.

I turned my head in the direction where I assumed my assistant to be. Two men in neon-colored jackets were bent over him. I saw his chest rising and falling. At least he was still alive. And suddenly my breath came much easier.

Once Raphael was convinced I would not try to walk out, he let go of me and settled down on the floor.

"Don't you have anything to do?"

"Officially, I'm not even here."

Logical. "And what are you not doing here?"

"Maria called me."

Maria … of course. I had not really expected her to stay home patiently waiting for my return, right?

"And then you rallied the troups to come and save me?"

He made a face. Possibly a grin. I could not see it too well from where I was lying. "This will have a rat's tail of paperwork. Fortunately the Dutch are less stern when there's an emergency."

"And they get all the praise for catching an international smuggling organization."

"Yeah, that, too. All that's left for me is writing long reports." He opened the Velcro of his Kevlar vest and let it drop on the floor.

"By the way, I still think that Kuipers is involved", I said.

"The shipper? Van Haren offered him to us on a silver platter the moment they gave him fancy bracelets."

So he had not gotten away. "Did you find some white powder on him?"

"Drugs? No." Raphael shook his head.

I had to do everything myself. I groaned as I sat up.

"Wait!"

This time I was prepared and ducked under Raphael's outstretched arm. I limped towards the gate and out into the sunlight.

At least a dozen official-looking vehicles were parked between the buildings on the customs area. I walked towards one with POLITIE written over the side. The neon orange stripes threatened to blind me. One of the officers in heavy armor was about to close the back doors.

"Wait", I asked in English, "do you have van Varen inside?"

The man looked at me nervously. What was wrong with him? Only when Raphael stepped next to me, he gave a brief nod.

"Could you open once more?"

"Just do what she asks", Raphael interfered.

Together they opened the doors and dragged van Varen into the light. The man was pale, his suit wrinkled. I looked at his feet – finally his shoes had gotten dirty! This brought me a weird sense of satisfaction. He made tiny steps, for his feet were chained as well. I leaned forward and put my hand in the inner pocket of his jacket. He flinched.

Nothing.

"Where did you put it?", I asked and looked him in the face.

He blinked. "What are you talking about?"

"The white powder." Maybe that would help his memory.

"I have seen no white powder."

"Don't play games." I stepped up so close to him that the tips of our noses almost touched. "You have seen what happened to your pet."

Hearing these words, van Varen seemed to shrink. "I threw it away. Inside the warehouse."

Without another word I turned and stepped through the gate once more. This was where he must have stood when the police arrived. I squinted and looked around. Maybe the sachet had slid under one of the boxes … I opened my shields with care and groped for the memory.

There it was. As expected. Under one of the crates.

Raphael, who had followed me, frowned. "Don't touch it, that's evidence." He waved a Dutch colleague over and instructed him to secure the powder. The policeman took plenty of pictures with his camera before he went down on all fours to get the sachet. It was put in another plastic sachet and labelled.

"Tell him to have it examined by a magic consultant."

"There's none around. But they have called one to the police department, he will look at it later."

"This powder is magically enhanced", I explained. "Van Varen used it to draw a circle of protection."

Raphael was surprised. "Is it really that easy?"

"Sure, why not? If a professional made it, even a drunk duck could use it."

"Kuipers doesn't care about magic, from what I know." Raphael thought about it. "This means that there may be even more people involved." He looked at van Varen, who had followed our discussion with a nervous expression. "Come on, let's go and ask him."

"I swear, there's no one else!" Van Varen was shaking with fear. I wondered whether his crimes could be considered "magic-related crimes".

I turned to Raphael. "What about Goldilocks?"

"Who??"

"That guy … you know, from university. Did he say anything?"

Raphael looked at the floor. "The merman got him."

My memory only caught on after a moment. The tank. The spell. The blood. Of course. "How unfortunate."

Raphael stepped aside. "We should not talk about this freely", he urged. "Strictly speaking, you have killed someone using magic."

So that was why everyone was giving me the nervous eye. "It was self-defense!", I said.

"You will have to talk to Madame Santé." When he said that, he sounded worried.

Talking to Madame Santé, that fit my plans beautifully. I turned around and saw Falk limping towards the gate, supported by two paramedics. He was pale as death.

I addressed the policeman who had put van Varen back into the van. "You did not happen to find a pentagram? Silver, with a leather necklace?"

He nodded and added, "Sorry, it is evidence. We will send it your way as soon as our investigations are complete."

Too bad. I would not see it again any time soon. Maybe I should get one as a tattoo, just in case.

As all things had been settled, I ran after Falk. "Are you finally done with your tough guy game?" I had trouble not letting my relief show.

"You think you should be talking like that?", Falk asked. He could not use his right leg properly. The remnants of his clothing were drenched in blood.

I turned towards the paramedics. "Does he have any bite wounds? They said the asanbosam was venomous."

The woman shook her head. "Only shallow cuts and bruises. But his knee is sprained pretty bad."

Best news in a long time.

Getting us patched up took a while. The police cars with van Varen and his helpers were gone towards the police department already. A hearse had come to collect Goldilocks. As the shock wore off, I felt the pain and the exhaustion. This strange energetic cocktail had done for me, really badly. I dreamed of sleeping for three days straight. But first I had one last task to take care of.

"The authorities have agreed that you can talk to Madame Santé back at her place", Raphael said and led me over to his car.

"But I have to get the car back to Annegriet!", I protested.

Falk sighed. "I'll take care of that."

"How are you going to find her?"

"No problem", Raphael interrupted. "We checked her license plate and found her address. A boat at Oosterdok." He gave Falk a slip of paper. "I have asked an officer to drive you, your knee is quite messed up."

Was he planning on leaving me alone again? "Wait! Where will I find you later?"

"I'll take you to him as soon as the interview is over", Raphael promised and held the door for me.

The whole thing did not feel quite right, but what was I supposed to do? I sighed and got in Raphael's car.

Traffic in Amsterdam is not for the faint of heart, believe me. Maybe not as bad as Paris, but the number of bikes flying through the streets alone turned our trip to Madame Santé's magically secured skyscraper into an adventure. When the car was finally tugged into a tiny space across the street from the building, I had to pry my fingers off the door handle. From the passenger seat the trip had looked quite different.

He looked at me. "You know this is serious."

No, that was completely new to me. "I thought this is just an interview?"

"In cases where magic is involved, Madame Santé is judge and henchwoman in one person. If she declares you guilty, it's game over for you."

"How is that possible? I am not even a Dutch citizen!" Besides, hadn't that been enough excitement for a day?

Worry was plain in his face. "This is an argument we might use to get you off the hook. It's why I have come as well."

"I do not need to be saved", I replied. He was starting to annoy me.

"But you need someone who knows the rules." He leaned toward me. "I don't want to harm you, promised! Besides, your secretary is going to kill me if something happens to you."

Good point. "Then let's see that we get this done."

The doorman examined Raphael's badge as if he was sure it was fake. He had not been this thorough when I was here for the first time. Then he called the top floor and talked briefly before he let us pass. The elevator was as quiet as the last time. It seemed smaller, though. Or maybe that was just because I was being nervous. Raphael's breath was extremely loud and annoying next to me. Then the carpet swallowed our steps, and we approached the door with the dried chicken feet. It was slightly ajar, but there was no smell of food. I was not sure whether that was a good or a bad sign.

Madame Santé sat at her table and seemed to be waiting for us. She was wearing a tight black dress with a waterfall of black cloth pooling around her feet, and a complicated purple silk turban on her head. In a bowl in front of her she was burning dried leaves. Next to it she had placed a rattle adorned with tiny bones. The instrument looked like a heirloom, scratched and worn. "Under normal circumstances I do not hold these meetings at home", she purred.

"We are very grateful for your kind offer." Raphael made an effort to sound friendly and polite.

Madame Santé had the quickest of glances for him. "You can wait outside."

Raphael shook his head. He did not like this idea. But what was he going to do? The heads in front of the window showed how powerful this woman was. He shook his head, looked at me again and closed the door behind him on his way out. Once again I was on my own.

Madame Santé waited until I had sat down. "They told me on the phone the things you have done."

"Self-defense."

"You have used the Old Energies. No one from outside has ever done this." She seemed puzzled.

"Is that what you want to talk about?" I was surprised. "It was an emergency reaction. I am not even sure I could reproduce it."

"Yes, of course, you have been marked." She held her hand out. "Take my fingers and tell me what you see."

I hesitated. "What about the interview?"

"You are glowing."

This could not be. Although – I listened to my inner voices. Something had changed. Like a second heartbeat, completely synchronous with my own. I took her hand and waited.

Nothing happened.

Yet the voodoo priestess was satisfied. "The Old Energies do not lie. Your mother has trained you well."

And that even though I had no magic heritage. The praise must hurt her. I increased my concentration, tried to hold and shape the second heartbeat inside my chest.

And suddenly I knew. "You gave van Varen the powder."

Madame Santé's expression derailed. "What are you talking about?"

"The powder for the magic circle. No one in this city would be reckless enough to magically connect to criminals such as these. They are all afraid of you."

"Is that what you see?" After the first fright she seemed more curious than afraid of the things I knew.

I hesitated. I had not really seen it. It was more like knowledge suddenly manifesting inside my head. "Aren't you afraid someone may find out?"

"How could they? The powder has long gone." She tilted her head, looking at me.

"But why did you do it?" I did not understand. "And why did you get me a permit?"

"The spirits are watching you. They told me you would not rest. I had to give you something and hope that you would not dig deep."

My head started pounding. "I still don't get the connections."

212

She leaned forward. Her clothes smelled of incense, perfume and sweat. "Look deeper."

I tried, but I came up empty. After a few moments I shook my hand in frustration and let go of her hand.

"Fine, I'll tell you. I had a sister. She did not care about the Old Craft. Instead she married a rich German. A shipper."

I had not seen that coming. "Kuipers is your brother-in-law?"

She nodded. "And the father of my niece. The last in a long line of priestesses. She is fifteen."

"That alone is no reason to do something this stupid!" On one hand I felt it was not good if she told me this much – possibly she did not intend to let me go. On the other hand, I had to know. While we were talking, I tried to secretly collect a ball of red energy under my skin.

"He and I don't get along well. But we had a deal: I help him with his tiny rituals, and in return I get to train my niece once she turns twenty-one."

Rituals – that must be the fights we had witnessed. That would explain the traces of energy I had found clinging to the first dead fighter. "What are these rituals good for?"

Madame Santé looked at me as if I was particularly dumb. "Do you know anything about German economics? Do you know what most shipping companies are going through?"

"So this is only about money?" I could not believe it.

"And about the family heritage. My brother-in-law hopes that the future husband of my niece will take over the family business. However he has to keep the enterprise going this long. The fights are part of a complicated agreement."

Blood magic. I shuddered. "Good thing we straightened that out. And now I had best be going. It's several hundred kilometers to Riverton."

The voodoo priestess smiled. It was not a friendly smile. "Oh, I do intend to let you go. If you can go, that is." She grabbed her rattle and started weaving a complicated rhythm.

The room seemed to melt around the edges. My gaze was glued to the heads. Their mouths moved in soundless unison. Come, they seemed to whisper. I noticed that I had gotten up from my chair and was walking in their direction. I did not remember starting to move. Desperately I groped around in my insides for the energies I had collected, but they seemed to sleep. I had covered half of the distance to the window. And what would happen then? Would I jump? Or would the heads somehow turn me into one of their own? I did not know what frightened me more.

Deep beneath my feet there had to be what Madame Santé had called Old Energies. I had used them by chance just hours ago. Now I was searching for them, begging – and when I had the idea to entice them, they came. Like a gush of fresh spring water they filled me up, and suddenly I knew what I had to do. She is a liar, I thought. Formed the words in my head and sent them on their way with the Old Energies. Let them flow into the heads. Breathed life into them.

214

"Liar", they whispered. Maybe it had only been the wind. The force that had dragged me to the window disappeared. "Liar, liar!" The whisper grew. It echoed from the walls, hissing and growling like an angry rattlesnake hiding between the furniture. I turned and took a step in the direction of Madame Santé.

The priestess was turning grey in the face. Her gaze flickered from my face and the heads lining her windowsill. A blue glimmer was dancing across her dress.

I pointed a finger at her. "Liar!", I shouted, and the heads followed.

She fell to the floor as if her strings had been cut, and I was free.

I left the apartment without turning around. Behind me the heads continued whispering. "Liar … liar!" I knew how to silence them, but I did not do it. Instead I approached Raphael who made an effort to look relaxed, waiting with his back against the wall. He did not look happy.

"Are we done?", I asked. "Let's go."

"That was quick." He looked at me quizzically.

I did not know what he had heard. Not too much, I hoped. "Sure." I nodded. "Come on, I don't want to think about the whole thing any longer than necessary." I grabbed his arm and dragged him to the elevator. "I am too glad if I never have to think about voodoo or cryptids ever again."

Epilogue: Weekend getaway

Maria and Falk were waiting for us at the Oosterdok. I almost stumbled down the step into the water, blinded by relief. I gathered myself and embraced my secretary. "Thanks for calling Raphael. You saved our lives."

"You thought you'd get rid of me this easily, didn't you." Maria smiled. "I had this inkling that you would try to get rid of me once things get interesting. Fortunately, I had this handsome guy's phone number in my phone." She nodded at Raphael.

Was he turning red or was I only imagining things?

Falk was sitting on a wooden chair, leg extended in front of him. He was drinking coffee from one of Annegriet's colorful mugs. And there she was, my savior, balancing a tablet with more coffee mugs. "I thought we could all need a hot drink. It's such a lovely day!" She winked at me. "I will read in the papers what happened to you, right?"

By the way … "What are they going to do about the cryptids?", I asked Raphael.

"I guess they will send them to various zoological institutions. The university here in Amsterdam has declared willingness to organize everything."

That was something. I thought about all the exotic lives, forced into tiny boxes, and I was glad that they would find a home soon. They were safe, and the illegal fights would stop. That was all I had to know at the moment.

For a while we drank our coffee in silence. Then Raphael handed his back over to Annegriet, thanked her and said, "I think I'll get back to Riverton. There are forms waiting for me to be signed."

Maria frowned and looked at me. "What about you two lovebirds?"

I glanced at Falk. "I think I would like to stay for a few days. Who knows when I'll get here the next time."

He nodded. "As long as you don't make me jump through burning hoops …"

"You are giving me great ideas!" I raised a finger in mock salute.

"Would you be so kind to drive me back to Riverton then?", Maria asked Raphael.

This question surprised all of us. I watched his face turn various different shades in rapid succession. An insecure smile spread over his cheeks. He wasn't … was he? "My car … I don't know …"

"You can use the transporter Helena and I took to get here. And your car stays with these two." Maria's voice did not allow for any objection.

But Raphael did not look as if he was suffering much. He grabbed the car keys from his pockets and handed them over to Falk. "Here, have fun." Then he and Maria left and disappeared down the street.

I looked at them. Raphael's broad back and his blond short hair, next to fragile Maria in her wheelchair. I hoped it worked out … Ah well, they were adults. They could take care of themselves.

"Do you want to go and find a hotel, or are you sleeping at my place?", Annegriet asked once the others had disappeared from our view. She did not take no for an answer. "From here you could have a great time exploring the city."

This sounded like a great idea. And once we had had enough, we could always sleep under one of the countless bridges, watching the stars. There were some adventures from my wild years left I wanted to tell Falk about. But not today, and not all at once. He did not yet know what he had gotten himself into.

THE END

Thanks

There are many people who helped me turn the first ideas for "Whispering woods" into a complete novel. This time I would like to thank the readers first – everyone who wanted to know what happens to Helena, Falk, Maria and Strega, everyone who keeps buying the books and leaving comments for me.

Stephanie went on long hikes with me to gather enough pictures to describe the places where the action is. She also helped with her invaluable input during various stages of writing and editing. And she made the wrath you can see on the book cover.

Bianca did the same, looking out for mistakes, always asking about what would come next and keeping me in my seat when I did not feel like writing.

Jonquil helped me translate the book, catching stupid typos and grammar glitches and all kinds of things only a German would say or understand. If there are still mistakes in this manuscript, they are mine and mine alone.

The cats – well, they are cats. They sleep in my office, destroy the cables of my devices and sit on the notebook ouwhen they think I've been writing enough and should take a break to feed them. For this I should thank them as well, I guess.

And of course I also, always, would like to thank Richard, who supports my writing habit and probably hopes I leave all my words on the pages so he does not have to listen to them over breakfast. I love you!

In case you can't get enough – here's where to find me:

http://diandrasknusperhaus.org

Or come and find me on Facebook: Diandras
Knusperhaus

I love hearing from my readers – reviews, fan mail and
funny pictures from around the world! And in case you
know anyone you think might like the world of Helena
and Falk, send them my way. And now something
completely different: Advertisement!

Magic behind the mountains

Helena Willow, witch and magic consultant, is thrown into a series of serious events when she hires former inmate Falk as back-up to talk to some bad guys. Together they keep solving magic riddles and hunting evil, with the support of Helena's personal assistant Maria and her black and red cat Strega. Meet witches, satanists, trolls, gods and zombies in and all around Riverton by reading the following adventures:

All Souls' Children – a quest for a missing witch and her unborn child in the mountains around Riverton.

Mirror Lake – examining the deaths of non-human children in an orphanage across the country.

Skinned – a mysterious woman forces Helena to help her get rid of her ex-husband, endangering her own children and Helena's family.

Aetherhertz

(Anja Bagus)

Germany: Baden-Baden 1910

Since the turn of the century a mysterious green fog rises from the rivers. Æther is a blessing for industry, a curse for humans. Airships conquering the skies, monsters roaming the river banks.

In fashionable Baden-Baden all still seems well with the world. Yet, while bathing guests from all over the world take their leisure along the avenues and in the Kurpark, young women are dying of a mysterious poisoning.

While trying to get to the heart of this, Fräulein Annabelle Rosenherz finds herself in great danger, because she is hiding her own secret.

Join Annabelle Rosenherz: uncover a conspiracy, experience first love, and suffer along with her when her secret threatens to destroy her life.

Mabel Bunt and the Masked Monarchs

(B R Marsten & R Collins)

Mabel Bunt, harlot and commoner, is sent to entertain a young lord on his last night before execution. When she leaves his cell she finds herself a fugitive wanted by the Crown and caught up in the schemes of a stranger who

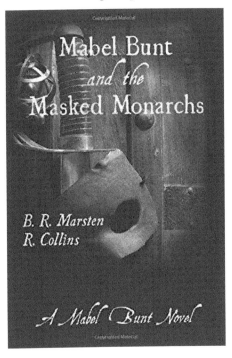

seeks revenge from behind the faces of dead kings. This is the first of the Mabel Bunt novels, with Mabel, our harlot turned hero, corset-deep in a clockpunk adventure filled with masks, intrigue and swashbuckling fun.

14934415R00128

Printed in Poland
by Amazon Fulfillment
Poland Sp. z o.o., Wrocław